"Don't touch me," she hissed at them, baring her teeth like a cornered animal, as they grabbed her. She'd always hated being grabbed, held down . . . the bad memories replayed in her head. Dad grabbing her, belting the shit out of her, kicking her when she was down. Only now Dad and Danny seemed to be one and the same confused image, and these two men were going to hurt her, too. With the slipperiness of an eel she broke free, raced along a passage and through some doors that led onto the balcony. Like a cat she climbed up onto the railing.

"Come near me and I'll jump," she screamed.

The taller of the two men grinned.

"We hear that every day, girlie. You won't jump."

She did.

CARE FACTOR ZERO

O

Margaret Clark

AVON
tempest

AVON BOOKS, INC.
1350 Avenue of the Americas
New York, New York 10019

Reprinted by special arrangement with Random House/Australia
Library of Congress Catalog Card Number: 99-95319
ISBN: 0-380-81390-4
www.avonbooks.com/tempest

First Avon Tempest Printing: March 2000

Printed in the U.S.A.

OPM 10 9 8 7 6 5 4 3 2 1

Dedicated to Kerry Ford, who works so tirelessly with young people; to Claire Carmichael, who suggested the title; and to Mark Macleod, who always has faith in my writing.

Written with the help of Kerry Ford, who provided much of the research material for this novel, *Care Factor Zero*.

CARE FACTOR ZERO

one

THE baby cried, a pitiful, plaintive sound in the small flat.

"What's wrong with the kid now?" groaned Danny, his head splitting and his tongue feeling like he'd chewed the neighbor's cat.

"I dunno. Probably hungry."

Tess snuggled farther into the pillow, pulling the covers over her head. Danny opened a bleary eye and looked at her, or rather at the red tufts of spiky hair sticking out like a scrubbing brush.

I'm sleepin' with a scrubber, he thought fleetingly, then felt a pang of guilt, because he and Tess were an item. They had Larceny, their beautiful baby, who was now bawling her eyes out. He poked Tess hard in the ribs.

"Fix her up."

"You. It's your kid, too."

"Do it!"

He gave her a harder jab, then suddenly pushed her

violently in the back as she curled away from him. The baby yelled louder as Tess swore and landed on the floor with a thump.

"Pig! I don't feel well."

"Just feed the kid, will ya?"

Tess staggered over to the carry cot and lifted Larceny out.

"God, she stinks."

Roughly she took the screaming baby through to the kitchen table, pushing a load of empty take-out boxes, beer bottles, and overflowing ashtrays out of the way as she dumped the baby down.

"Where's her diapers, Danny?"

"I dunno. In the corner."

"The packet's empty. There's none left."

"Okay, so there's none left. Use a towel or somethin'. Only feed her first, will ya?"

Holding the baby like a sack of spuds under one arm, Tess staggered across the kitchen, opened the fridge, found a half-empty bottle of formula, and shoved it into Larceny's mouth. There was silence as the hungry baby sucked greedily at the cold milk. Danny propped himself on an elbow and focused on the pair.

"Aren't you s'posed to warm that milk?"

"Yeah, well, she's drinking it, isn't she?"

The baby finished in record time. Tess thumped her on the back vigorously, nodded with satisfaction when there was a loud burp, put the baby back on the table, and took off the soiled diaper.

"Yuck. She's all red."

"Put on some powder, then, fix her up and come back to bed." Danny's voice had deepened with desire as he watched Tess moving round dressed only in a rather grubby T-shirt that just covered her bum.

"Don't get ideas," she said, putting the baby, now swaddled in a towel, back into the carry basket. "I'm not in the mood. I've got a pain in my guts and in my head."

"You've always got a pain in your guts. Or a headache. Or you're too tired."

"I wasn't too tired last night."

"Yeah? I was too wasted to remember. Come on, over here."

"No. I'm going in to Emergency. I feel bad, Danny. You'll have to mind the kid." Her green eyes had clouded over, and she was lost again in her own miserable world.

Danny fell back against the pillows and sighed. Tess was always moaning about some part of her anatomy. She was still wearing a dirty bandage around her wrist because she was sure she'd sprained it when she fell down a flight of steps coming out of JoJo's, and she was sure she had some terminal disease, AIDS, leprosy, you name it.

At first when she'd got pregnant it had been a big mess. Her old man had raised the roof, said she'd behaved like a slut, belted her, and chucked her out. They couldn't go to her mother because she was living somewhere in Sydney and didn't want to know Tess anyway. Or so Tess said. They couldn't go to his old man's because he liked little kids too much, which was why Danny had done a runner five years ago. So they'd rocked on into Social Security and spun some shit.

Welfare had found them this flat, the kid had popped out, and everything had been great. For a while. Donations of the carry cot, pram, baby clothes, food, and furniture had rolled in from the Salvos. The flat looked great. People in the street would stop and admire Larceny in her pale pink clothes or bright trendy gear.

"What's her name?" everyone would ask.

"Larceny."

"Larceny?"

"Felonious taking away of another's personal goods with intent to convert them into one's own use." Danny and Tess would recite with a grin. They'd both heard the phrase often enough in juvenile court. It had a nice ring to it. Larceny. Original. They were both sure that there wasn't another kid in the country called Larceny.

At first Tess had been rapt to have the kid to care for: She said it made her feel important. But lately she'd been moaning about feeling bad, her head always ached, her guts ached, the place was a dump because she never cleaned it, the baby kept bawling, and life was one big bummer. Last night they'd taken Larceny in her carry cot to a party and both got drunk out of their brains. They'd smoked a lot of dope, too. It always seemed to make Tess morbid. Danny could vaguely remember his maniac mate Tarri driving them home.

He blinked and looked round the flat. Clothes were piled in the corners, shoes were scattered everywhere, and the three cats which Tess had adopted and kept feeding scraps were asleep on the clothes. It had looked great when they'd first moved in, with the two fat armchairs and a sofa, a small TV, the double bed with its bright floral cover in their bedroom, and the kitchen with their teak laminate table, black-vinyl-covered chairs with the tubular legs, fridge, and stove. Playing house, that's what they'd been doing, but it hadn't lasted long. Carting a baby all over the place was boring, and the time they'd left it home the neighbors had called the cops because Larceny had bawled and bawled, and the cops had called Welfare, and Welfare had said, "One more chance."

"No appropriate role models," Danny had heard the social worker say to the cop. "What can you expect?"

"What's all this crap about role models?" he'd said to Tess later on, when they were watching TV. "We've got the kid, we're looking after her, she's guzzling milk by the quart and growing like a weed, what do they want?"

"I dunno."

Tess had stared at the TV screen with a fixed expression on her face. She always seemed to do a runner into her own brain whenever things got too hard. And lately she'd been getting worse.

"Right, I'm outta here," Tess announced suddenly, jolting him from his yesterday-thoughts back into the harsh reality of the moment.

She'd dragged on some jeans and sneakers and was heading for the door. Danny threw back the covers and leapt out of bed.

"Hang on, where do you think you're goin'?"

"Told ya. Hospital. I'm feelin' real crook. I've gotta go, Danny."

Her strange green eyes were huge pools in her white face. She looked real spacy. Danny felt a coil of fear in his guts. He had to do something. She wasn't allowed to run away, put herself in the hospital and leave him with this mess.

"Yeah? That's what you think," he snarled.

He grabbed her arm and shoved her roughly back against the wall. Her head banged on the plaster with a dull clunk.

"You're stayin' here!"

"Danny," she whined. "I gotta get to the hospital. I told ya, I don't feel well. I . . ."

"Stop ya moanin'. There's nothin' wrong with ya," yelled Danny, feeling angry and frustrated. Somehow he felt responsible for her and the kid, and when she acted like this he couldn't cope. She was letting him down. He slammed his fist into her face and blood spurted all over his hand.

She screamed, flaying out with her arms, trying to protect herself, and the sight triggered off something in Danny, something deep, like a movie being replayed, his mum cowering against the wall while his old man laid into her, and it all got mixed up as he punched Tess in the stomach and the head. She crumpled at his feet in a small ball. He gave her a kick for good measure. The baby wailed loudly.

"Get out, then, and take this little shit with ya. Go on."

He grabbed up the squalling baby and threw her hard at the blubbering heap of Tess on the floor. She clutched the baby as she staggered to her feet, wrenched at the door handle, and lurched through the door, slamming it behind her.

"Good riddance," muttered Danny, going to the table and draining the last drops from a beer bottle. "Who needs you anyway, you stupid slut!"

Tess ran from the flat, clutching the baby. Blood dripped from her nose onto Larceny's feathery head, but Tess was oblivious to this. She hailed a taxi.

"Are you all right, love?" asked the elderly driver, when he saw the blood. He handed her a wad of tissues.

"I need to go to the hospital," she said woodenly, as Larceny bellowed her lungs out. "Oh, shut up, SHUT UP!"

She shook the baby roughly, which made her yell even louder. The taxi driver bit his lip and planted his foot on the accelerator. He didn't want any trouble, and this was

Trouble with a capital T. He screeched through the streets, pulling up with a squeal of brakes as they reached the hospital.

"Hey. What about my fare?" he yelled, as Tess flung the door open and hurled herself out, still clutching Larceny. She didn't answer as she lunged through the doors of Emergency. The taxi driver shrugged. You win some, you lose some.

"Help me," whimpered Tess as she reached the counter.

"Name?" asked the woman, glancing at her, then back at her paperwork.

"Tess Leyton."

"Have you been here before?"

"Oh, for shit's sake. Can't you see I'm dying?" cried Tess dramatically.

"Address?"

Tess flung the baby onto a nearby seat. Whirling, she ran for the stairs.

"Hey. Come back. You can't . . ."

Tess raced up the stairs, two at a time, her heart pumping madly. She wanted to find a nice, white-sheeted bed to lie down on, and have a nice, kind doctor give her some painkilling injections, get rid of the pain in her guts and her head, and send her into quiet oblivion. She didn't want any major grief.

Two orderlies got her at the top of the second flight of stairs.

"Don't touch me," she hissed at them, baring her teeth like a cornered animal, as they grabbed her. She'd always hated being grabbed, held down . . . the bad memories replayed in her head. Dad grabbing her, belting the shit out of her, kicking her when she was down. Only now Dad and Danny seemed to be one and the same confused image, and these two men were going to hurt her, too. With the slipperiness of an eel she broke free, raced along a passage and through some doors that led onto the balcony. Like a cat she climbed up onto the railing.

"Come near me and I'll jump," she screamed.

The taller of the two men grinned.

"We hear that every day, girlie. You won't jump."

She did.

Larceny Leyton strode down the street, head high, hips swinging suggestively in her tight 501s. Freedom. Cutting school was the only way to go. Age fifteen and her thirteenth school, nothing different. Same desks, same types of teachers, same types of kids, same old routine, only in different suburbs or different towns. Eight foster families plus ten stays in residential care and two in an adolescent psych hospital had left their mark on Larceny. So had the knowledge that her mother had committed suicide by flinging herself off a hospital balcony in Melbourne. Wimped out. Couldn't hack it. Well, there was no way Larceny Leyton was going to kill herself: There was too much living to do. That was how she felt today. The demons hadn't come into her head for weeks, the ones that told her to hurt and lash out. Or kill herself. They'd gone, she was in a new residential that wasn't a total shithole, and everything felt good. Larceny Leyton was alive and well. The rest of the world could go to hell.

A number of Welfare people and foster families had tried to change her name. They'd said Larceny wasn't a proper name! It was indecent!

"NO!" Larceny had been adamant. It was the only legacy she had from her mum and dad. No photos, no mementos, nothing. Only the long red hair, green eyes, and swarthy skin, a most unusual combination from the coupling of Tess and Danny. Slim body, long legs, and an attitude.

She'd finally tracked down her dad, an alcoholic, living with the woman who was now her stepmother. There were two small stepsisters whom Larceny hated with a frightening intensity. Feelings of absolute rage engulfed her when she looked at them. She wanted to hurt them. Staying there had been horrible. She'd wanted Dad to herself, but he was a weak man, and she despised him for this and the fact that her stepmother was a controlling, manipulative martyr who saw Larceny as an unwanted intrusion, a reminder of a past life in which she had played no part. And she was a misfit there. Too bright. The shrinks had given her IQ tests, and she was way above average, in the gifted bracket, they said. Not that it had done much good, being gifted with a high IQ.

"Hey! Larce!"

It was Emma, a twelve-year-old street kid she'd befriended. Emma was totally off her face on the cheap cask wine she downed in copious amounts. Larceny frowned. Emma didn't look good. There was stale vomit down the front of her denim jacket, and her eyes looked spacy. There was more than wine in her guts.

"What are you on, kid?"

"Huh?"

Emma's eyes rolled in her head. Her skin was pale and clammy, and her short dark matted hair was damp with sweat. This was not good. Larceny dragged Emma over to a bench and went through her pockets. An empty Avil packet was crammed in one pocket.

"Did you take this stuff?" Larceny demanded, shaking Emma back and forth like a rag doll. No answer.

"Shit!"

Larceny knew an overdose when she saw one. What to do? She didn't need major grief and aggro just then; she was heading down to the beach to meet up with Jane and Cathy. They were planning to do over some shops and get some new gear. Larceny wasn't called Larceny for nothing, and she had a rep to maintain.

"Everything all right?"

Larceny looked up as she tried to support Emma's lolling head. A cop stood there staring at them both. She was young and earnest-looking, probably just out of cop school. Her beaked hat was pulled down low, practically perching on round, wire-framed glasses, and she had a thickset body on short, stocky legs.

"Yeah."

Larceny didn't need cop trouble.

"Your friend doesn't look too good," said the cop, bending to take a closer look.

"She's just . . . the flu, ya know."

Cheap wine fumes hit the cop's nostrils like a blast from a brewery, and she narrowed her eyes.

"I think your friend needs medical attention."

"Yeah, right."

Larceny gave up. If the cop took charge, she'd be free to go to her rendezvous. But Emma'd never forgive her for handing her over to a cop. There would be hospital, inquiries, serious shit. Well whose fault was that? Not hers. The cop felt for a pulse on Emma's thin wrist then frowned. She unhooked her mobile and dialed.

"Can you send an ambulance immediately to the Mall? I've got an OD here."

She pushed Larceny to one side, loosened Emma's collar, laid her along the bench, and started pressing on her chest.

"Hey. Come back here," said the cop, but Larceny, back straight and head up, was striding away on her long legs. She never got involved. She was a loner, used people like Jane and Cathy when she needed them, and trusted no one. Not even herself. That was life—when she wanted to be bothered living. Sometimes she didn't.

There was a mass of scars on her arms, cuts going the right way down the veins, not across, but never deep enough to finish the job.

She walked quickly down the main street toward the beachfront, turning along the esplanade to take a shortcut round the sailing school, where she knew Jane and Cathy would be waiting.

"What kept you?" asked Cathy with belligerence.

She was a dumpy lump, dressed in baggy jeans that had seen better days, and an army-surplus duffel coat. Her round face was creased with disapproval and her eyes narrowed as she surveyed Larceny. *Thick as pig shit,* Larceny thought with satisfaction. She liked gathering a crew round her who were not very bright. It made her feel superior. She was the leader, and she didn't like being challenged.

"Cop trouble," she said.

Cathy looked scared. She didn't like cops. Or anyone else in authority. She was always in trouble at school for nonattendance, and so was Jane. They were a good pair, gullible, eager to please Larceny, and, therefore, easy to manipulate.

Jane scuffed the toe of one dirty sneaker in the sand. She was thin, almost to the point of emaciation, with a sly, foxy face, mousy hair, and a bad attitude. She was street smart but not overly bright, couldn't read or write despite her years of schooling.

"What happened?" she asked.

"That kid Emma. Wine and Avil. OD'd in the Mall," said Larceny shortly. Emma's plight was already fading from her mind. She needed to get these two organized. Thursday was always busy with shoppers, which made shoplifting easier. The stores had frantic staff, who were occupied keeping customers happy, and Larceny needed clothes not only for herself but she had some orders to fill. Good 501s, quality tops, computer software, perfumes, cosmetics, underwear . . . there was a ready market.

"We'll do Mayer first. They've got an inventory sale. Go for the dark colors so the dyes won't be bad if we have to bust them off, and I need size ten and twelve jeans."

Cathy grinned as she opened the duffel coat, revealing a number of pockets sewn into it. Jane was swinging a large carry bag by its handle.

"Let's go."

Larceny strode off, with the other two scurrying to keep up. They crossed the road from the beach, walked along a street, up an alley, and reached the back entrance near the food hall of the busy shopping plaza.

"Okay, you know what to do."

They entered the rear doors of the big Mayer store, which was humming with activity. Larceny had already sussed the place the day before, noting where the security cameras were and what the stock looked like. It was her job to act suspicious and draw the eyes of the staff and security guards so that the other two could do their work.

She strolled right through the store up to the perfumery and liberally squirted Sunflowers on one wrist. The assistant glared as Larceny fingered the different items, picking them up, glancing around casually, moving herself out of view, selecting one or two perfumes with a studied casualness, holding one close to her pocket then replacing it on the counter. It was a tantalizing and convincing act. Out of the corner of her eye she saw the security guard beginning to circle.

Larceny wandered toward the lingerie, conscious of the eyes watching her and also conscious of Cathy and Jane moving swiftly to the perfume counter. She fingered the lingerie, held it up, stroking the satin sensuously, then replacing items on the racks. She moved away, looked at some other items, then casually returned to her first choices. Picking up a delicate pair of briefs, she strolled to the counter.

"How may I help you?" asked the shop assistant, looking like she wished she didn't have to acknowledge Larceny's presence.

"How much?"

"Twenty-five dollars," said the assistant, looking superior. "There's the price tag on the garment."

"Twenty-five bucks for *this?*"

Larceny tossed the garment on the counter. Security circled, waiting and watching, as Cathy and Jane took advantage of the moment to stuff a number of items in bags and pockets, well out of range of the cameras.

She strolled across to the jeans piled on tables for the sale, fingered a few (they were the ones that Cathy and Jane would nab later) and detoured to the Teen Shop. She repeated her fingering/admiring/glancing-around process, ducking her head and averting her eyes when she met those of the security guy, who'd now been joined by another. They waited and watched like stalking wolves as she moved to the jewelry, selecting pieces and trying them on. Out of the corner of her eye she could see them practically slavering as she slipped some earrings into her pocket, then, as if shocked at what she'd been absentmindedly doing, she replaced them on the rack. Cathy and Jane should be over at the designer tops by now. Larceny yawned, looking at her watch. A stroll back to hosiery should just about do it. She got there, looked around, pretended to notice security and the watching eyes of half a dozen staff who'd been following her progress through the store, and walked swiftly to the exit. If she was challenged there was nothing on her, not one item. They didn't.

She headed up the street toward Johnny Rockets. Shoplifting was thirsty work. She needed a Coke and a cigarette. Ten minutes later Cathy and Jane joined her, looking triumphant.

"They are all total losers in there," said Jane, opening her bag to reveal the contents. "Easy."

"Yeah. Easy," echoed Cathy, her coat bulging.

Stupid cows, thought Larceny. *Without me they'd be sprung straight off. They're getting too confident. Time I dumped them anyway.*

Suddenly, she felt the grayness descending on her. It was like this, coming out of nowhere for no apparent reason. She shook her head, trying to clear it.

"You okay?" asked Cathy.

"Yeah. Look, we'll dump the gear for now behind Youth Works. I'll wait till it's quiet, take it to Sammy, and give you your cut later, okay?"

"What about the rest? The computer stuff?"

"Later."

"But . . ."

"I said 'later'!"

"You look kinda sick," said Jane, peering suspiciously at Larceny as she held her throbbing head in her hands.

"Yeah, I don't feel too good. Might have been the skunk I smoked last night, okay? Let's go."

They dumped the stuff behind some big bins, and Larceny said she'd meet them two hours later when the heat had died down. Not that there was any heat, stupid bitches, but they believed her. The grayness was swamping her brain, and any moment the voices would start, teasing, tantalizing, tormenting. She knew she wasn't mad, it was just the effects of the skunk she'd smoked. Had to be. She should stay clear of the hydroponics and go for the home-grown variety of dope.

As soon as the others were out of sight, she gathered up the goods in a couple of green plastic garbage bags she had stuffed in her pocket and lugged it down the street to Sammy Soul's Pawnshop. It was top gear and should be worth a bit. He had jewelry, cameras, electronics, and the regular goods up front, but he was a good fence for the designer stuff and perfumes she'd just nicked.

Instead of going in the front door, she sidled warily round the back and did the prearranged four sharp jabs on the doorbell. Sammy himself opened the door, his bald head with wispy tufts of graying hair, pointed nose, and shrewd darting eyes making him look like an oversize rat. Larceny blinked and tried to stay with it, though the voices were starting to take over her brain. He *was* a rat: He was turning into one before her eyes.

"Get him! Go on, get him," mocked a voice in her head, the same one that compelled her to try and hurt the stepsisters.

"No time to deal. Hundred bucks the lot," said Sammy, peering in the bag she'd put on the ground.

"Aw, come on. That lot's worth at least five, six hundred," she said, trying to fight the mist, trying to stay in control.

"A hundred. Take it or leave it!"

Larceny was filled with a wild, consuming anger. She blinked, trying to clear the gray clouds, which were becoming fiery red before her eyes like a blazing furnace.

"Get him!" screamed the voice in her head. It shrieked through her brain, making her wince.

"You . . ."

Rage roared through her like an inferno. The steal was worth at least six hundred, maybe more. He was trying to rip her off. Sweat broke out on her forehead, and she saw his rat-face leering at her, teeth pointed and sharp. In her mind he was coming at her, going for her neck. Larceny was still holding the other bag. With a phenomenal strength she swung it hard at his head. He crashed into the iron security door, blood gushing from his scalp as he crumpled at her feet. She dropped the bag, staring at the blood. He had to be dead, no two ways about it.

"Kick him. Kick him," screamed the voices in her head.

"NO!" shouted Larceny, holding her hands over her ears. She turned and ran blindly away, as if pursued by all the devils in hell.

two

LARCENY got off the train, hiking her tote bag over her shoulder. She'd risked going back to the home for it, cramming it with her meager possessions. Then she'd made her way to the railway station and caught the first train to Melbourne. She felt in her coat pocket. Ten bucks left. Ten bucks to start a new life. Not enough. She'd have to get some deals going in this city, and soon. But first . . .

She walked out into the street, straight up to a newsstand, and picked up the evening paper. Scanning the headlines, she saw that there wasn't anything about the murder of Sammy.

"Hey. No free reads. Pay up or put down," said the woman minding the stand.

Larceny turned, froze the woman with a scathing look, and tossed the paper carelessly back on the pile. The woman shrank back from the cold hatred in Larceny's eyes. This one was bad.

So. Nothing about Sammy. Too early yet. Good. It would take the cops a while to track down the source of the stolen goods and round up Cathy and Jane *if* they were smart enough. And by the time those two spilled their guts . . . this was a big city, with plenty of places to hide.

She strolled up Flinders Street, sussing out who was hanging round under the clocks. She knew Melbourne, knew where the street kids lived, knew some of them from her stays in homes and the psych hospital. She winced as she remembered those black days. Uncontrollable, they'd labeled her, when she'd attacked one of the night nurses. The woman had been a pig bitch, a bully, who'd bossed all the inmates around, was handy with her fists, and taunted them with malicious innuendos. After that the night nurses were all scared of her. She'd attended classes, psych groups, and individual counseling during the day, but every night she was escorted to a youth refuge. The workers there were cool, laid back, and didn't give her any aggro. She'd kept to herself, stayed in her room, remained mute, and eventually they'd given up trying to get brownie points by being the ones to "cure" her.

Larceny grimaced. She knew she wasn't mad. None of the psychologists and psychiatrists could put a label on what was wrong with her, and it had pissed them right off. Bipolar? No. Manic-depressive? No. Schizophrenic? They weren't sure.

She'd shown them. She'd been cunning, playing their games. Shrewd observation of the signs and symptoms of mental illness had allowed her to mimic the different conditions. She had the shuffle, the pacing, the muttering, rocking back and forth, the craziness down to a fine art, and just when they'd thought they had her for straitjacket material, she would be clear, calm, and normal.

She'd started smoking dope when she was eleven, and she knew that if she smoked too much, or used the potent skunk she'd hear the voices. Lots of kids did. Saw things, too. So much for marijuana being a nice mellowing-out drug. Well, it did mellow her out, mask the shit, but the voices . . . She'd seen some kids get the same effect when they used LSD, magic mushies, or datura. Drug-induced psychosis, one psychistrist had said when he'd seen Mikey totally out of his tree on datura. Mikey. Nice kid. *Wonder what happened to him?* thought Larceny. He was about the only human she'd ever really related to, ever really liked.

He was kind of innocent and gentle. They'd boiled up the lilies they'd nicked from the psych-hospital garden. Typical, growing trumpet lilies in a psych-hospital garden, showed how dumb the doctors were. She'd been all right when she'd swigged the mix, hadn't felt much apart from a mild buzz, but Mikey had thrown a serious psycho, and they'd had to lock him up. She'd been regraded to a residential home, never saw him again.

Larceny went up the steps under the clocks and into

the foyer of the railway station. People were hurrying round her, intent on their business, oblivious to the young girl with the wild red hair, strange icy green eyes, and tight, pale face. She dug out the ten-dollar note from her pocket and bought cigarettes, a packet of chips, and a Coke. Then she moved over to a wall, dropped her tote bag at her feet, and turned, surveying the scenery, smoking, and sipping the Coke.

After a while she felt someone was watching her. She turned her head slightly. There was a guy looking at her. He was leaning against the wall, arms folded across his chest. He was wearing an expensive-looking black-leather jacket that hung loosely from his slight frame, and tight black trousers. His dark eyes surveyed her curiously. Mid-thirties, Larceny thought, though nowadays it was hard to estimate ages. Thirteen-year-olds could look thirty, and sixty-year-olds, with the aid of cosmetic surgery, could look thirty. But you could usually tell by the eyes, and Larceny had lots of experience studying eyes.

He was swarthy, lean, and mean. She met his eyes coldly. He didn't look away. He unfolded himself from the wall and sauntered over, hands linked into the top of his belt.

"New in town?"

His voice was deep, low, and sexy. She'd seen his type around. He was a pimp on the prowl for new talent, Larceny decided, although why was a bit of a mystery, seeing as girls were dropping out of the sky to go on the game. Easy money. They thought. Stupid bitches. It was a fool's game, prostitution.

But this was cool. She'd play along, get some money out of him, then bail out. There was no way she was going on the game for some pimp. If she was ever going to have to resort to selling her body, she'd be in charge of doing it, although she was sure she'd rather be dead first. The thought of anyone touching her made her freeze. It always had, as long as she could remember.

"What's it to you?"

"Thought you might need a friend."

"You?"

There was scorn in her voice, and she tossed back her head mockingly, the mane of red hair swinging like a soft curtain against the wall behind her. The man narrowed his eyes. This wasn't the usual run-of-the-mill, gullible yet street-smart babe he was used to conning. Most of the street kids, male or female, were desperate for affection, for someone to care about them, to get some permanency in their fragmented lives, which made them malleable and easy prey. This one was different. Fire and ice. He wondered if she was worth the trouble, but she was interesting. Challenging. Intriguing. He put on his most winning smile.

"Hungry?" he asked.

"Hardly."

She indicated the empty chips packet at her feet.

He grinned, enjoying the game. She was smart, this one.

"Cold?"

"Hardly."

She shrugged in the thick plaid jacket.

"Lonely?"

"Hardly." The green eyes flickered over him, and a faint smile tugged at the corner of her mouth. "You're here trying to give me grief, aren't you, so how can I be lonely?"

He put out his hand. "I'm Nick Farino."

She looked at it, rejecting the handshake, and he dropped his hand to his side as his lips tightened. He wasn't used to rejection. He didn't like it.

"Look, man, I'm not interested in whatever you've got to offer," she said curtly. "Do me a favor and piss off."

Nick Farino wasn't accustomed to being told to piss off, especially by a mere kid. He scowled.

"I run a business," he began.

"Not interested. I told ya, piss off."

"I need a receptionist."

"Oh, perlease!"

"I do."

"I can't type."

"You don't need to type, you need to answer the phone, make bookings for the clients, that sort of thing."

Larceny looked at him and decided to taunt him a bit.

"You a doctor? Or a dentist? Or what?" she asked demurely.

He didn't answer, just looked back coolly, not rising to the bait. He was a very sharp operator. She changed tactics.

"The world's full of receptionists busting to work, so why me?"

Nick Farino shrugged.

"Dunno," he said, which was the first honest word he'd uttered for about a year. And he didn't know. She drew him like a magnet, not in a sexy way, in fact she was more of a turn-off with her cold, blood-freezing eyes and her aura of icy anger. But he wanted to know more about her. She fascinated him.

"Look, man, thanks for the offer, but I don't want to work, okay? I'm just cruising through."

A knock-back. He couldn't take it. He was tempted to grab her, twist her arm up her back, and frog-march her down the street to his car. Babes usually fell all over him, and this one he wanted to control because somehow she was turning the tables and controlling him. He stepped toward her.

"Don't even think about it," she said softly but menacingly, as the city commuters bustled and jostled around them. He stopped short, frowning.

"Wait here!"

With long strides he walked away toward the entrance and zapped down the steps. Larceny leaned back against the wall, bemused. She wasn't frightened of him. When you'd been mauled by orderlies, pinched by nurses, pricked and poked at by doctors, yelled at by teachers, given grief by cops, moved in and out of a bunch of foster homes, and given the works by court magistrates, fear of people was almost unknown.

But she was afraid of being shut up, caged in juvenile for killing Sammy. She was scared stiff of being slammed back into a psych hospital and doped up with antidepressants. She was terrified of losing her freedom, of being confined by walls and bars. No human could get emotionally near enough to her to be a threat, she made sure of that. Just the walls and bars . . . She could feel the gray mist beginning to swirl up, seducing her thoughts, nagging and niggling, and soon the voices . . .

"Right, kid. This is Stella."

Larceny blinked, bringing herself out of the fog. Nick stood before her half-dragging a skinny old woman with a wrinkled face like a monkey, dyed black hair, and a harassed expression.

"This your number one babe? No wonder you're desperate," said Larceny sarcastically, though her curiosity was aroused.

"Stella runs the hot food stall across the street," said Nick impatiently. "I've decided she needs an assistant. You."

"This is crazy," said Larceny. "Are we on *Candid Camera* or something?" She crossed her eyes and put out her tongue. "Where's the hidden camera? Wait, don't bother answering, I've wasted enough time hanging round this place. I'm outta here."

She hefted the tote back up from the floor and went to barge past Nick, but his arm shot out to grab her elbow. She froze. She hated being touched. The ice-fire came into her eyes, and Nick, seeing her look, dropped his arm like it had been seared on a hot plate.

"Don't ever, ever touch me," she said softly, her eyes narrowed like a cat's.

Stella spoke.

"The job. No strings, no trouble. Cash in hand."

Larceny looked at the old woman. She gazed back. A tough old bird, shrewd and hardened with years of struggling against the odds.

"Why me?" she asked simply.

"You've got spirit. And you're not going to rip me off!"

"You're the only one on this planet who thinks so," said Larceny. "My name's Larceny, and larceny's my game, man. Got to live up to my name."

Stella chuckled. "Nothing to rip off except donuts, pies, and hot coffee, luv. Are you coming? I've got Jack minding the stall, and he's not exactly the full falafel, if you get my drift."

Larceny gave herself a surreptitious pinch to make sure she wasn't dreaming. Or tripping out on the aftereffects of the skunk. No, she was here at Flinders Street Station with a smoothie called Nick and a scrawny old woman called Stella who'd just given her a job. This was for real. Sammy Soul was the bad trip, the nightmare. She sighed.

"Yeah. All right. Just for tonight, and no hassles."

Following Nick and Stella, she walked out into the rain-spattered street as the sky darkened, heralding a cold wintry Melbourne night. People scurried past, heads bent against the rain, eyes down, never smiling at each other in apology as they bumped shoulders. *Like a mob of sheep,* Larceny thought, *all going somewhere, following the leader to the trains that will take them home to their safe, warm houses where they'll eat, watch TV, and tumble into their beds before they get up again the next day and repeat the same commuter process. Caged within the oppression of their routine, mundane lives like circus animals. Forget it. Not for me,* she thought.

They crossed the road and reached the stall. It was more or less just a hole in the wall. Upon seeing Stella the old dude called Jack unfolded himself from a stool, nodded, and shuffled off up the street.

"He's a man of few words. Dump your gear there," instructed Stella, pointing to a corner. Larceny dropped her tote bag and took off her coat. It was warm and steamy in the booth.

"Right. This is how you make the coffee. Donuts and pies are in the warmer."

Stella wasn't exactly overflowing with the gift of the gab either, Larceny thought with a small secret smile.

Good. She liked quiet types. Meaningless chatter got on her nerves. She'd heard enough of it in the psych wards. That, and pompous psychological jargon.

It was basic. Easy. You put coffee in Styrofoam cups, pies and donuts in bags, and took the money. The clientele was rough, street-tough—the misplaced, the lost and lonely dregs of the city who couldn't afford more than a coffee and a donut.

"I do sandwiches and rolls in the summer," Stella confided, as Larceny served an old drunk with shaking hands and rheumy eyes who coughed and wheezed as he handed over a two-dollar coin.

"Yeah. Right."

A few streeties rolled up, hard and unforgiving faces glistening in the rain, feral in their denims, the product of a society too busy dealing with enterprise bargaining, key performance indicators, and an ailing economy to deal with its ailing youth, its human flotsam and jetsam. They cracked a few jokes with Stella when she gave them a couple of donuts and charged them less than the usual because "the jam's gone and leaked outta them."

"Who's the babe, Stella?" asked one of the guys. He had long black hair slick with raindrops and a sharp, intelligent face. He moved with the dark grace of a panther as he lounged against the booth.

"None of yer business. Hands off," snapped Stella.

"Larceny," said Larceny, who resented Stella's verbal intrusion.

"Huh? Where?"

The guy swung his head round as if he expected to see an armed bandit charging up the road loaded with stolen goods.

"Me. My name. Larceny."

"Yeah? Cool. Mine's Lynx. See ya."

"That young buck's trouble," said Stella, watching Lynx dart in front of a car, then back onto the safety of the sidewalk as the car driver jammed on the brakes, sending the car skidding sideways.

"Yeah. So am I," said Larceny under her breath. But she wouldn't give Stella any aggro: The old woman had given her a job, hot food, and coffee during a lull in the passing food traffic, and was now preparing to close up her stall. It was close to midnight.

"Here's your pay."

Larceny looked at the notes in her hand.

"Four hours. Six bucks an hour. Twenty-four bucks."

"Yeah. Right."

Larceny pocketed the money.

"Got somewhere to sleep?" asked Stella.

"No. But I'll find somewhere."

Stella seemed to be considering. Then she shrugged.

"If you're still around tomorrow, there's work here after five, okay?"

Larceny watched as she pulled down the heavy steel roller door and locked it. Had Stella been offering her a bed? Pride stopped her from asking. Still, sleeping on the streets was nothing new. She'd been doing it for years in between foster families that hadn't worked out and residentials that hadn't worked out, either. Sometimes the streets were the safest places to sleep!

Without further good-byes Stella shuffled off down the street and round a corner, clutching her leather handbag tightly to her chest. It was a miracle that someone didn't mug her senseless and take her money, Larceny thought, but then if she was under the protection of Nick Farino, maybe the word was out, and no one wanted to tangle with Nick. He looked like he'd be bad news if crossed.

Hoisting her tote bag onto her shoulder, Larceny walked wearily across the street and into the sanctuary of the Flinders Street Station. Dark shapes lay swaddled in coats and blankets, their worldly possessions in bags scattered around them against the walls. More flotsam and jetsam, unwanted, unloved, and dismissed. Since the closure of most of the big mental asylums and refuges the mentally ill, nicely termed the "intellectually impaired," wandered the streets, confused and bewildered, unaccustomed to this frightening freedom. And society, unaccustomed to seeing weird and deviant behavior on its streets, chose to ignore the problem.

Larceny lay down in the only available space beside one of the snoring bundles and hoped she hadn't inadvertently taken someone's patch. She was physically aching all over from bending into the pie warmer and standing on the hard concrete of Stella's stall for hours, and mentally and emotionally exhausted from being on the run from the law. Was it only hours ago that she'd murdered Sammy Soul? It felt like years.

Feeling timeworn, weary, and utterly alone, Larceny pulled her tote bag under her head for a pillow as she closed her eyes and fell into a fretful sleep.

three

"YOU ready for breakfast?"

Larceny groaned as a toe prodded her in the back. She opened one sleepy eye and focused on a pair of shiny leather shoes. Traveling up black tight jeans and a white T-shirt topped by a loose jacket, she met the dark-eyed stare of Nick. She struggled to sit upright. Every bone in her body ached from lying on the concrete floor, and she winced as she got to her feet. All round her bodies were moving, groaning, muttering, and coughing the graveyard hawk of the living dead.

"The cops will be here soon to move everyone out," said Nick, his eyes raking over her as she stood, slightly swaying on her feet.

"Cops?" said Larceny, feeling panic well up like bile in her throat. Her eyes darted to the newsstand and the morning papers. She'd temporarily forgotten about Sammy Soul.

"Yeah. Cops. It doesn't look nice for the general public to see all this lot."

He jerked his thumb at the moving mass of humanity, which was gathering belongings and shuffling out into the bleak wintry morning.

"What are you doing here?"

"Told you. Taking you for breakfast."

"Why me?"

"Do you always argue so much?"

He grabbed Larceny by the arm. She tried to pull back, but he gripped her even tighter.

"I told you, don't ever touch me," she hissed.

He ignored her. She looked round. One old guy was staring at them. When he saw the agonized look in Larceny's eyes he dropped his gaze and busied himself picking up his belongings. She flicked her eyes at the others. No one was interested: They had their own problems. Well, she'd play along, then as soon as he relaxed his guard, she'd take off. She was good at playing this game.

"Where are we going?" she asked, walking meekly beside Nick as he steered her round the human baggage that littered the station.

"You're coming to my place for a shower and breakfast. Then we'll talk."

"Forget it!"

Larceny stopped and faced him, her eyes cold.

"Grow up, kid. I'm not going to eat you. Or come on to you. You stink!"

His sharp words made her realize that she hadn't had a shower for two days. Ashamed, she turned her head.

"Come on!"

Unresisting, she let him lead her down the steps and out into the chilly gray world that was Melbourne city on an August morning. His car, a black sporty-looking model, was parked at the curb. Opening the door on the passenger side, he waited till she got in, then slammed the door shut. Suddenly, Larceny felt that she couldn't care less where he was taking her and what he was going to do to her. She was too tired to fight. He pulled away from the curb and headed away from the city, not speaking.

"Where are we going?"

"I told you."

Larceny wondered whether she had enough energy to jump out of the car. That would be the sensible thing to do. But as if reading her mind, he planted his foot even farther, rounding the corners on two wheels. Larceny gave up and huddled farther down into her seat. She decided to take note of where they were going so she'd know how to get back to Flinders Street.

He headed down St. Kilda Road and swung the car into Domain Road. On the left the park was gloomy, misted with rain, and the benches were empty. It was too wet and cold for even the most seasoned vagrants to sleep under their newspapers. Nick threw a right into Park Street, then another right down a small side street with barely room for the car. He zapped the car into an even narrower side street and pulled up at the back of a block of flats.

"Where are we?" she asked, as he held the car door open.

"I told you. My place."

"But where?"

"South Yarra."

Larceny grimaced as she looked round. A posh suburb. A very swish neighborhood, quiet and dignified. From another side street she could see into the main street, where big old trees were growing on the edge of the sidewalk. She didn't belong here. But then neither did this Nick Farino, either. She knew his type. He'd cheated and scammed his way here, a smoother Sammy Soul with a few more brains.

She thought quickly. She'd play along, have a shower, eat breakfast, then bail out, even if she had to kill him to do it. She'd already killed one man, poor dead Sammy, so another wouldn't make any difference.

"In here."

They went up some steps and Nick punched numbers into the security pad near the door.

"Frightened someone's gonna break in and knife you while you sleep?" asked Larceny with heavy sarcasm.

He didn't answer but ushered her into a foyer.

"My flat's upstairs."

They went into the lift. He pressed the button marked

"3" and they whizzed up to the third level. The lift doors slid back.

"In here."

He inserted a key into the lock and opened the door. It led into a hallway. Pale beige floor tiles. Paintings on the cream walls. Nice.

"The bathroom's through there."

He gestured down the passageway. Toting her bag, Larceny went where he'd indicated, her sneakers making no sound on the tiles. She tried one door. Inside was a bedroom with a single bed and a number of boxes heaped against one wall. It didn't look lived-in. The next door opened onto the bathroom.

It was unreal. There was a big spa bath with gold taps, a hand basin, and a shower, all in white with cream-and-gold trim. Black-and-fawn towels were neatly folded over towel rails, and there was a collection of men's toiletries on a glass shelf above the hand basin. Larceny was tempted to have a spa bath, but resisted the idea. A quick shower, a change of underwear, something to eat, and she was out of there.

She stood under the steaming shower soaping her hair with Sassoon shampoo. Luxury. She smoothed shower gel all over herself. Nice. She wished she could stand under the soothing water all day. Forever. It saved worrying about the scum of her life when she could just stand there and watch it disappearing down the drain.

But there were still things to do. She had to confront

Nick Farino. He was as good as his word in that he hadn't barged into the bathroom and tried to come on to her. But he was still a slimeball. It was written all over him in Magic Marker.

Climbing out, she toweled herself briskly, put on clean underwear, a shirt, and jeans, rolled her soiled clothing into a ball, which she stuffed into her bag. Slinging it over her shoulder, she went back down the hallway to find Nick.

Her nose led her to the kitchen. He was standing at the stove. A golden brown pancake was sizzling away in a frying pan. With a deft flick Nick flipped it onto the stack he'd made, which were piled on a bright blue plate.

"Sit down."

He pointed to the table, which was covered by a blue-and-white-checked cloth. It was set for two, with delicate white crockery and gleaming silver cutlery. Two cane chairs with pale blue cushions were placed one at each end of the table.

It was a dream of a kitchen, bright and sparkling, the woodwork on the cupboards glowing richly under the soft lighting. A divider separated the cooking area from the eating area. It was massed with lots of healthy-looking plants.

"I can't imagine you with a mop and bucket," said Larceny, as she sat down and looked round at the sparkling sink, ice white appliances, and general air of squeaky-clean.

"It's a serviced apartment."

Larceny gathered he meant that someone cleaned it.

He put the piled plate of pancakes on the table and sat down opposite her, with the expanse of table between them.

"Eat!"

She picked up her fork and gazed through the glass sliding door that led onto a balcony. Through the trees dripping damply against the gray sky she could see the outline of tall city buildings. It was like being in a nest amongst the forest of buildings.

"Syrup?"

"Thanks."

He passed her the container.

"Do you want your coffee now or later?"

"Now, thanks."

He got up again and brought the percolator to the table. He poured a cupful and passed it to her.

"Milk? Sugar?"

"Thanks."

It was like she was on a date in some posh restaurant or something. Nick sat down again and regarded her quizzically. She bent her head. She didn't want to look at him, or have him staring at her while she ate. She always hated people doing that. It was probably a hang-up from some of the foster homes. They'd watched like a hawk to make sure she ate everything.

"No sweets till you've eaten all your veggies, dear."

Or, "You should be grateful that you've got food when there's all these starving people in the world." Or in the psych hospitals, watching to make sure you did eat, and weren't on some starvation kick.

There was a rustling sound as Nick began to read the morning paper while he forked up his pancakes. Larceny started eating one. It was delicious. She kept forking them off the plate and had wolfed down three before she'd noticed what she was doing. She blushed. He'd think she was a pig.

But then who cared?

She stole a glance at the top of his head. He rustled the paper as he turned a page. Larceny squinted at the headlines. Her heart gave a thump. Sammy Soul! Was his murder going to be splashed across page one? She frowned, peering at the page and trying to read upside down. Nick suddenly put down the paper, making her jump.

"You want to read it?"

"No. That is—"

He folded the paper and passed it over, watching her intently. Larceny picked it up and opened it, skimming the first four pages.

Nothing! Didn't murder make headlines anymore? She felt vaguely disappointed. Then felt a faint ray of hope. Maybe Sammy Soul wasn't dead after all!

Nick sat watching the play of emotions across her face. She fascinated and intrigued him. An ice maiden, cold and unemotional, yet he'd seen her apprehension as she'd scanned the paper, sensed her relief when she hadn't found what she was looking for. Maybe she'd thought her disappearance would be in the paper? He'd met a hundred babes on the run, possibly a thousand. He reckoned he was a good judge of character. Some of them were thick, some blatantly sexy, some shrewd and smart. He only chose a handful to work for him, and always moved them on after several years. There were other "houses" to take them in. No intravenous drugs, that was his rule. It got messy. He hadn't seen Larceny's arms: She had them well covered. But she didn't have the look of an addict. Maybe she was a recreational?

"So?" he said. "Ready to talk?"

He leaned forward, chin on his hands, regarding her impartially as if she was a butterfly impaled on a pin.

"No."

"Pity. I thought a shower and breakfast would loosen your tongue. Well, I guess I'll just phone the cops and get them to come and pick you up."

He saw raw fear leap into her eyes as she automatically closed her hand round her fork, the nearest weapon she could find. He saw her reaction and was pleased. They were so easy to manipulate when they were running scared.

I'll stab him if he tries to turn me in, Larceny thought wildly. Gray mist swirled before her eyes and, raising the fork, she gripped it tighter. She glared at him.

Nick saw the fury in her eyes. The fork was raised higher.

"I'll kill you if you try to call the cops," she hissed, standing up, poised to lunge with the fork. She couldn't kill him, but she could take out one of his eyes. He knew he had to be cool. Any sign of fear from him, and she'd strike.

"Give me the fork."

"No."

He put out his hand, palm upward. Larceny raised her arm. She looked at him, ready to plunge it down hard on his hand if he showed any fear, but his face was expressionless. She leaned over the table, her face an angry mask, and raised her arm higher. His eyes followed her arm and widened slightly as he sucked in his breath. Then he immediately seemed to gain control of himself. He leaned forward.

"Give me the fork."

His eyes stayed on her face. Unfathomable dark eyes met stormy green.

"No!"

"GIVE ME THE FORK!"

His voice was devoid of expression and thus controlling in its unemotive tone. Suddenly, with an angry resistance, she dropped it into his outstretched hand. He'd won!

"That's better."

Defeated, she slumped at the table, warily watching to

see what he would do. But part of her felt triumphant. The gray mists had come, but there had been no voices. The anger had been born of her own volition. So, she was not defeated! She'd lost the battle but won the war. With herself. She straightened her shoulders and faced him.

"What do you want?" she said.

"Not what I first thought," he said coldly. "I was going to give you a job. But you're too unstable."

Larceny smiled. She was calm, rational, cool.

"Unstable? I don't think so. Work for you? No way!"

Nick felt confused. She was completely sane at the moment, back in control of the situation and herself. Maybe with a few Valium he could keep her calm, but then she'd lose the fire, and that was her attraction.

"What's your name?"

"I thought I told you. Larceny."

"Larceny what?"

"Larceny Leyton."

"How old?"

"Fifteen. Look, what is this, twenty questions? I'm outta here."

"Relax. Do you smoke?"

He didn't mean cigarettes. He uncoiled himself, went over to a drawer, and pulled out a small carved box. Inside were neatly rolled reefers. He proffered the box.

Larceny blinked. She could almost feel the mellowing-out, the taste on her tongue.

"It's top stuff."

Tempted, Larceny stared at the box.

"Go on, take it," said a voice in her head.

"No!" she snapped, pushing the box away.

"You don't do drugs?"

He sounded surprised.

"No."

She thought of all the shit she'd used in the past, dope, alcohol, pills. And the junk they'd stuffed into her when she'd stayed in psych hospitals: Valium, serapax, ritalin, injections of modecate when she'd gone off the planet. And lithium. All of it had made her dopey and controllable, but it hadn't got rid of the bad thoughts in her head. Or the anger. Or the bitterness.

"Nothing at all?"

"No. Cigarettes, coffee, some alcohol. Not that it's any of your business!"

"Most runners are into drugs."

"Who said I'm a runner? Who said anything? Just leave me alone, will you? I don't need you or anyone else!"

She jumped to her feet and grabbed her bag.

"I'm outta here. Now!"

She thought he'd try and stop her, but he didn't. He just sat watching her with his brooding dark eyes, as she hoisted her bag, wheeled, and headed for the door. She expected him to follow, to grab her, to shove some narcotic into her arm. He didn't move.

She stormed down the passage to the front door. Expecting dead bolts or some complicated device, Larceny was surprised when the handle turned easily in her hand. She swept down the steps into the street, pausing to gaze up briefly through the rain at the apartment building. He was standing on the balcony looking down at her, the roof sheltering him from the rain.

"Loser!" Larceny mouthed up at him, and did the famous one-finger salute. Then, turning her back, she headed off down the street.

Nick smiled to himself. She could run, but it wouldn't do her any good. Eventually he'd track her down through his vast network, which stretched like tentacles through the underworld. He was a powerful man with powerful connections. The little shit thought she'd beaten him, but he had her name. Her age. He'd find out more about this Larceny piece. And then, when he was ready, he'd reel her back in. He'd changed his mind. He could use her. Some men would find her instability exciting.

He went back to reading his paper. Something had thrown her when she'd been reading it. His curiosity was piqued. Where had she sprung from? What was her history? Dressed up in the right gear, she'd be a stunner. She was very clever. He liked that. He tossed the paper down and went to make a phone call.

Larceny kept walking through the driving rain. Her jacket soon became sodden, and her hair hung in damp strands round her head. She walked with determination toward the city, down Domain Road, across St. Kilda Road, over the bridge, and back through the misery of a wintry Melbourne day to Flinders Street Station.

It was the only home she had.

She took off her jacket. It was cold. She was better wearing the wet jacket than not, so she put it on again. She wandered up and down, bought a magazine and a cup of coffee, though she wasn't really hungry. It was just something to do. She looked at her watch and sighed. It was only nine. How was she going to fill in the day? Maybe suss out a few stores? Or get a bus down to St. Kilda beach and look at the sea for a while? In the rain? Nah.

She headed off across the street and spent the next few hours walking and watching, going in and out of shops, fingering the goods just for the hell of it, buying a burger when she finally felt hungry. She found herself gravitating back to Flinders Street Station again. Loneliness gripped her like spiteful pincers round her heart. No one knew her, no one cared. Well, she didn't care about anyone, either. She had money in her pocket, food in her belly, and a roof over her head, if the cops didn't give her grief. Who cared if nobody cared?

four

"HEY, Larceny!"

Someone knew her name? She swung round, and there was Lynx and several of the streeties, another guy and two girls. A nice, neat foursome. What did they want with her?

She faced them warily.

"What are you doing?" asked Lynx.

"Sun-baking, what do you think?"

He laughed, running his hands through his shiny black hair. He did it gracefully. A poser? He squatted against the wall, hunkering on his heels. The other three lounged, watching her, idly interested to see what would happen next. Lynx didn't usually chat up strays. It was out of character. One of the girls, short and dumpy, pulled out a packet of cigarettes and offered one to Larceny. She hesitated. Then she took it.

"This is Frantik."

He jerked his thumb at the tall rangy guy dressed in

denim who stood staring at Larceny. He had a shaved head and his scalp looked blue with cold. His eyes were darting all over the place. Coming down off something, Larceny thought; speed or maybe ecstasy. He swung a rucksack by one strap, back and forth, back and forth like a pendulum.

"This is Comma and this is Bex," said Lynx.

"I'm Comma," said the dumpy one.

The other one, spike-haired and tough-looking, flicked her eyes insolently over Larceny, then turned her head and kissed Comma full on the lips. *So that's how it is,* thought Larceny. Did it mean that Lynx and Frantik were an item, too? Not that she cared. Sex to her was taboo. It meant letting someone get physically close to her, and the thought was repugnant. Her sexuality wasn't an issue. She didn't know whether she was hetero, gay, or bi. If she had to define herself, she would've said asexual. Years of psycho-babble had taught her all sorts of terminology. Asexual. That was it. She didn't get urges and she didn't fancy anyone, not even herself!

"Where are you from?" asked Bex in a bored voice, deliberately draping her arm round Comma and thus marking her territory.

"Everywhere and nowhere."

Frantik nodded.

"I know that scene, man," he said. His voice was deep and gruff. Larceny frowned. She knew that name from somewhere . . .

"I've seen your work," she said suddenly, remembering the graffiti she'd seen on walls. "You're good."

"Thanks."

Lynx was still studying her through slitted eyes. She locked eyes with him. His nationality puzzled her. Greek? No. Maybe Puerto Rican? He grinned.

"Indian/Fijian," he said, reading her mind. "I'm the only one in Australia."

"How do you know that?"

"I'm the only one I've met, that's why."

"Come on," said Bex impatiently. "Let's go."

"Why?" said Lynx, still staring at Larceny. "What's your hurry?"

Bex looked bored. She whispered something to Comma, and they both giggled, looking at Larceny.

"We're going down to the beach. See ya."

They walked off, arm in arm. Frantik unfolded himself from the wall and followed. Lynx stayed put, hands on his knees, gazing up.

"Well?" he said.

"Well, what?"

"Coming to the beach?"

"In the rain?"

"Why not?"

He stood up. Larceny considered his question.

"Yeah, why not. I'm not doing anything else right now."

The others were waiting, huddled against the outside

wall like wet sparrows. In the gray light they looked pinched, defeated, and tired. The girls' faces had a white, pasty look that came from a diet of junk food, drugs, and bad living. Frantik had dark smudges under his eyes and deeply hollowed cheeks that gave his face an almost skeletal appearance. His hand shook as he lit a cigarette. Lynx looked like the only one of the three who still had life on the menu.

"You got any money?" asked Comma, looking at Larceny.

"Some."

"Enough for bus fares and maybe something to eat?"

"Yeah. Enough."

They straggled across the road, Larceny shivering in her damp coat, the others oblivious to the drizzling rain, and got on a bus heading along St. Kilda Road.

"How do we know if it's going to the beach?" asked Larceny, knowing that the buses went up Domain Road, Commercial Road, and other places away from the beach.

"This one is," said Bex, looking impatient. She held on to Comma's hand, then, meeting Larceny's stare, kissed Comma on the mouth again. Then she gazed round to see if she was shocking any of the commuters. One woman looked scandalized, several men looked amused, and the rest stared straight ahead.

Larceny looked at the commuters. Sometimes she studied people, wondering what was going on in their heads, where they lived, what they did all day long. It wasn't the end of a working day, so these were either shift workers or on the dole or rich retired. No, not rich retired; they drove cars or hailed taxis. They didn't catch buses. One woman, clutching four large plastic bags, rocked with the motion of the bus, gibbering to herself, a fleck of spittle on her lips. She looked dirty and unwashed, a piece of human garbage on a city bus. *Will that be me one day?* Larceny thought, shuddering.

"So," said Lynx, breaking into her thoughts, as Frantik looked out the window and Bex mauled Comma, "tell me about yourself."

"Why?"

"All right, all right. Don't get shitty. You don't have to, I'll tell you about me."

"What if I don't want to listen?"

Larceny didn't mind hearing other people's stories. Some kids could spin some good shit. But she never got emotionally involved. And she didn't like to reveal much about herself. People sometimes wanted to get closer: She didn't want that. She wanted to keep the walls up, keep them at a distance, not get too involved. Once she started showing any weakening or emotional need they would want something back from her, want more and more, emotional stuff she couldn't give. It was too scary. If you did begin to care about someone, they would ultimately reject you.

Hidden memories that Larceny couldn't erase began to

surface. Her dad. Those stepsisters with their big blue eyes, blond hair, and cute ways that made her want to throw up, to punch them, to hurt them for being Dad's little angels. That's what he called them. His little angels.

"Put your fingers in your ears, I don't care. I'm still gonna tell you about me anyway," said Lynx, butting into her thoughts, his chocolate eyes like deep river pools in his swarthy face. She'd seen river pools when she'd escaped from one of her foster homes. So nice, the Frasers, or was it the Wilsons? So many foster families; they got mixed up in her head. Then she remembered. The Wilsons. A regular Brady Bunch family. Christians. Good people. Didn't yell, didn't swear, sat at the table sharing conversation, sharing their lives with her. Only she didn't want to share.

"Why me?" she'd shouted at them when they'd tried to get too close, to get into her head. She'd picked up her roast dinner and flung it at the wall. The plate had shattered, spattering meat, vegetables, and gravy all over the place. They'd all stared in horror at the mess, then at her, fear in their eyes. That had made her even madder.

"Why can't you just get on with your lives and leave me alone?" she'd shrieked.

She'd rushed from the house, their fear shaking her last vestige of solidarity, their Brady Bunch niceness too cloyingly suffocating. She'd run through the park to the river and flung herself facedown on the bank. She'd stared and stared at the brown sluggish water until she was mesmerized. The treacle-deep pool below called to her seductively, luring her into its depths. Silently waiting, it reminded her of the brown sugar she'd once smoked in a cigarette. Chasing the Dragon, the Cambodian guy had called it. You felt a rush, then dreamy, seduced by the heroin, lulled into euphoria. The thick and syrupy treacle-pool promised a deeper oblivion.

"Larceny. *No!* It is not God's will!" Mr. Wilson had yelled, rushing up from behind and pulling her back from the brink.

"It's my will!" she'd shrieked, as he'd dragged her kicking and screaming back to the house. She'd rocked back and forth, muttering and gibbering, until the ambulance arrived to take her back to the psych ward.

Funny thing, that. You weren't allowed to kill yourself! Why not? Who really cared?

"You with me, Larceny?"

Lynx's voice shattered her thoughts, sending them scattering back into the dark recesses of her mind.

"Yeah, yeah."

"So, I decided that I wanted to get out of that orphanage and fast. I was going nowhere."

"What orphanage?"

"I knew you weren't listening. The orphanage in Fiji. Anyway, I read this magazine that said all these people couldn't have kids of their own and were desperate to adopt one. They mainly wanted babies, but there weren't enough to go round. Not Australian and American ones.

They were madly adopting kids with missing arms and legs, all that, so I thought, 'Hey. I'm good-looking and cute. I've got all my arms and legs. There's someone out there who's gonna want me.' So I put myself up for adoption."

Larceny focused on him, the dark thoughts pushed away. Adoption? He'd decided to be adopted?

"How old were you?"

"I told you. Six." She hadn't heard that part. She felt annoyed because she'd probably missed lots of interesting bits.

The bus bumped and lurched round the corner and stopped so the woman with the bags could get off. Larceny followed her with hooded eyes.

"That's you," said a voice in her head.

No. Please. Don't let me end up like that! She determinedly snuffed out the voice and dragged her thoughts back to Lynx.

"Did it work? Did you get adopted?"

"Yeah. A teacher at a private school and her dentist husband adopted me. They already had two kids, girls, but they couldn't have any more kids, and they wanted a boy. Cost them nearly thirty thousand, with documents, papers, passports, tickets. I know because they told me thirty thousand times."

"Least you know how much you're worth," said Larceny with a sudden grin that transformed her face from mundane to beautiful. "I'm worth nothing."

"I'm worth more if you add up all the private school fees, the violin lessons, horseback riding, snow skiing, sailing camps. Oh, rowing. And I nearly forgot a brief stint on the sax."

He grinned wickedly. "You see, dear Larceny, I'm an ungrateful rich little shit. I've had all this money spent on me. I've been adopted, given the family's name. On the surface I'm this Aussie called Marcus J. Manchester. But you see, deep down I'm still an Indian/Fijian called Imran Parjuda."

"But you've been here since you were six. Surely you can't remember much about Fiji?" said Larceny.

"I can't explain. There's this sort of tugging feeling, like you're in one place and you want to be somewhere else. Kids can be uprooted, but they still can't belong . . . well, I don't know about everyone else, but I can't."

"But you got what you wanted. You chose to be adopted."

"Yeah, well when you're six, you're not great at making life choices sometimes. I know I'm ungrateful, I've been told enough times. All the money spent on me, love and attention showered on me, and I still turned out bad. Isn't that a shame? Must be in my genes."

He shrugged, but his eyes burned black with anger.

"Why?" asked Larceny.

"Why what?"

"I still can't understand why you don't forget being born Fijian, just lap it all up, and live happily ever after."

"You ever tried being the only Indian/Fijian kid in an all-white household with two golden-haired white sisters, in an all-white school, in an all-white society?"

"But you couldn't have been the only dark-skinned kid," said Larceny. "Private schools are full of nonwhite kids. There's Asians galore."

"Asians are not black."

"Neither are you," Larceny pointed out.

"I didn't belong. I should never have left the orphanage. It was crappy there, but at least if I'd stayed in Fiji I would've been with my own people. Well . . . sort of, because I wasn't Fijian and I wasn't Indian, but at least I was in my own country. You can't know what it feels like. Forget it, we're here. Everybody out."

He leaned forward and poked Comma and Bex, who'd fallen asleep with their arms round each other, heads together. Frantik got up and swung himself down the steps like an uncoiling cobra, his rucksack bouncing on his back.

"His spray cans," explained Lynx, as they got off the bus. Comma and Bex followed Frantik, dancing like demons in the rain.

"Comma and Bex?" queried Larceny, her head cocked to one side as she watched them prancing about.

"Comma's not the full stop. Bex is one big headache."

Larceny looked puzzled.

"Bex powders. You know? Like aspirin. For headaches.

My mum lived on Bex powders. Teaching gave her one big headache, but she still did it."

"Why? If your dad was a dentist, she wouldn't need the money."

"It was her career. Her calling. And if she gave it up it meant she hadn't heard the right call, eh. And you can't admit if you've screwed up, can you, because if you live in that sort of world it's all fake anyway. To admit you've screwed it up means that you've got nothing left."

"That's deep," said Larceny in awe. "How old are you, anyway?"

"I told you before, but maybe you'd tuned out just then. Do you know that you tune in and out, Larceny? I'm not sure whether you're short-circuiting in your head or what."

Larceny felt herself closing up, shutting down. She did it whenever she felt threatened psychologically.

"Oh, no, don't disappear again into your brain."

Lynx looked dismayed, then suddenly he grinned with a Peter Pan charm. "Oh, do what you like. It's cool, babe."

His abrupt change threw her off-balance.

"Sorry," she mumbled.

"I'm seventeen, nearly eighteen. Supposed to be doing my final year. Then university. They've programmed me to be a dentist, only I can't stand the thought of looking at teeth. A dentist has to like teeth, don't you think?"

He grinned broadly, showing a mouthful of perfect white teeth.

"Do you go home to sleep or what?"

"Sometimes. I go home to get cashed up, then I bail out again when they start wanting to tote me around to shrinks. I've been to about five."

"I know that scene," Larceny blurted out before she could stop herself. Then she bit her lip. Shit. Why did she say that? Now he'd ask her a heap of questions.

But he didn't. He walked quickly down the esplanade, following Frantik, Comma, and Bex, leaving her to run, panting, after him. Did this mean he was rejecting her? Did he think she was a fruit loop? Anger welled in her like a fountain. She caught up, swung her tote bag from her shoulder, and started to belt him round the head with it.

"Whoa!"

He caught the strap and held on. They faced each other, stormy green eyes meeting angry black.

"What's with you now, Larceny? You nuts or something?"

The gray mist came down, cloying, evil.

"Get him," screamed the voices.

He saw the rage blazing in her eyes and intuitively recognized that anger masked her fear.

"Larceny. It's okay. Larceny!"

He knew better than to touch her. He ducked from the

swinging bag, but remained cool, while Comma and Bex stood frozen to the spot and Frantik looked frantic.

"Lynx. Grab her," yelled Bex.

"No. It's okay, it's just like a bad trip," soothed Lynx, his dark eyes never leaving Larceny's face. Her sleeves fell back as she raised both arms, and Bex and Comma both gasped as they saw the mutilations.

Larceny froze at their looks of pure horror. They knew! Defeated, all anger gone, she slumped down on the sidewalk.

"Look at her arms," whispered Bex to Comma. "She's tried to slash herself. She's psycho."

"Bex, shut up!" Lynx's voice was tight. "If you want to be useful, go and buy two hot coffees, black and strong, with lots of sugar."

"I haven't got any money."

"I have," said Frantik, eager to be away from the scene. "Let's go."

They took off up the street.

"Get up," said Lynx, not touching Larceny. "We need to get out of the rain."

Lurching, she got to her feet. She was so cold. Her teeth were beginning to chatter. She half stumbled to a bus shelter and collapsed, shivering, on the seat.

"Have you got any warm clothes in there?"

He indicated the tote bag.

"No. All dirty."

The others came puffing back with the coffees.

"Here. Drink it," he said, handing her one of the containers.

"But . . . I take milk, and . . ."

"Drink it!"

Larceny did as she was told.

"Now the other one."

The hot liquid scalded her throat, but it gave her strength, a caffeine burst that sent the blood pounding through her veins and made her heart pump harder. She groaned, closed her eyes, and leaned back against the wall of the shelter. The bursts of anger always left her weak. Her head throbbed with an aching weariness.

"Why can't you just leave me alone?" she muttered to the mocking voice that was chuckling in her head. The others thought that she meant them.

"She's crazy, man. A nutcase. Leave her," said Frantik. Comma and Bex just stared. Lynx frowned. He seemed to be thinking deeply. Then he sighed.

"I'll take you home," he said to her.

"Home? Your parents will freak," said Frantik.

"So what's new? They're always freaking. She needs a warm bed for the night."

"Yeah. Right. So do we all," said Bex sourly.

"We could take her to Sal's," Comma suggested. "There's no one in her room right now. Sal left with Lisa yesterday. She told me Bex and I could use it."

"You didn't tell me!"

"I didn't think of it, Bex."

"Sometimes you're a pain in the arse. Why are we freezing out here when we could be in a nice warm room with a TV?" snapped Bex.

"I forgot, didn't I?"

"Quit it. Let's get there. Fast," said Lynx.

"You're not bringing her!"

Their conversation whirled round the periphery of Larceny's mind like a damp, insidious fog. She was too drained to care what happened. So long as no one tried to get too close . . .

five

LARCENY woke up. She struggled to remember where she was and what had happened. Gradually her eyes grew accustomed to the gloom as she gazed round. She was on a sofa. Someone had put a pillow under her head and placed a moth-eaten blanket over her. She frowned, trying to remember. *What is this place?*

Then she remembered something about Sal and Lisa lending their room to Bex and Comma. This must be the room.

Up at the other end was a double bed. There were cupboards, a stove, small fridge and a sink down one side, and more cupboards on the other, with a single-size mattress propped against them. A TV on a low coffee table was on with the sound turned down low, and there was a rickety table and two chairs completing the furniture.

She knew real fear. How had she got here? Who'd brought her here? It was like a jigsaw with important pieces missing. She sat up and banged her head on a shelf that held CDs, magazines, and other paraphernalia.

"Shit!"

"You're awake. About time."

Bex uncurled herself from a heap of blankets on the double bed and looked sourly at Larceny.

"How long have I been here?"

"Since about two. You've been raving on, thrashing about, burning up. Lynx said you were delirious."

Bex got off the bed and came over to Larceny, putting a hand on her forehead. Larceny froze.

"Don't panic. You're not my type," snapped Bex, her eyes glittering. "I wouldn't want to get with you if you were the last person on earth."

She squatted beside the bed, her eyes level with Larceny's. "What's your game, sis?" she hissed. "You've got our Lynx goin' round in circles out buyin' food with Comma, and you've got Frantik out of his brain doin' your laundry down the street."

Under the blanket Larceny ran her hands down her body. She was wearing only underpants and a bra. Her eyes flashed with anger.

"Where's my clothes?"

"We took them off. You were soakin' wet. Just our luck you'd get real sick and die if we left you in them. Relax. There's hot food comin', clean clothes comin', then you're on your way, babe. We don't need you."

"Thanks," said Larceny dryly. Actually she could cope

better with Bex and her obvious dislike more than she could with Lynx and his kindness. Hatred, dislike, and loathing she understood. Caring and kindness was something else, something not to be trusted.

"Where's my cigarettes?"

"Probably gone through the wash cycle," said Bex. "I suppose you want one of mine?"

"Yeah."

"All take and no give, aren't you?"

"Yeah."

Bex passed over the packet and a lighter. Larceny lit up, inhaled, and nearly choked.

"What *is* this shit?"

"Regular tobacco. Sixteens."

Larceny's head swam. "I smoke fours."

"Well, sorry I can't oblige."

Bex sat back on her heels and stared at the wall, pointedly ignoring her. Larceny looked at her watch. *Nearly six! How could I sleep for so long?* Major anger and voice attacks usually left her exhausted, but never as bad as this before. Sammy's death, going on the run; the whole thing had knocked her about more than she'd realized. She looked at the top of Bex's head. Stuck-up butch bitch.

"So what's it like being a nutcase, then?" said Bex.

Larceny felt the anger beginning to boil, but forced herself to be calm. Bex was deliberately trying to wind her up. The other girl had moved to the other end of the sofa, sitting on the floor and leaning back against the armrest. Larceny smiled sweetly at her.

"It's cool. So what's it like being gay, then?"

"Huh?" Bex snapped to attention.

"You reckon I'm nuts and you're having it off with a girl. Now that's not normal, is it!"

"Mind your own business."

"No, you tell me. It is my business. You think I'm nuts. Not normal. You might be able to convert me, you never know," taunted Larceny. Bex looked at her coldly.

"I doubt it," she said. "Just lie there and keep your mouth shut."

"Maybe I should ask Comma."

"Do what you like, only right now *shut up!* I'm not askin' you about the cuts on your arms, am I?"

Larceny went rigid. Bex had hit a very raw spot.

"You had no right to strip me," she spat, her green eyes flashing hatred.

Bex yawned, pretending indifference, though her curiosity was aroused. The razor scars were numerous, showing that there'd been more than one attempt. Why had this babe wanted to bump herself off? There was more to this Larceny than met the eye.

"Yeah. Right. We should have left you lying in your wet gear. Anyway, we knew about the scars before we stripped you. When you were attacking Lynx and going psycho you put up your arms, and your sleeves dropped down."

Larceny froze. Then she remembered the look on Nick's face when she'd lifted her arm to stab him with the fork. She'd seen the widening of his eyes. He'd seen the scars, too. It made her feel very vulnerable.

"Can't even kill yourself properly, can you?" sneered Bex.

Right then Larceny decided to get her! She threw back the blanket and went to launch herself across the space, to gouge out Bex's sly eyes, to put her hands round that scrawny throat and . . .

Suddenly the door opened, and Lynx and Comma appeared, loaded up with grocery bags. Larceny, frightened by the force of her anger, fell back on the sofa and, suddenly conscious of her near nudity, pulled the blanket up to her chin.

"Did you rob a store or somethin'?" asked Bex as she surveyed the bags.

"Bread and groceries from the Salvos, some fruit, and we bought coffee, milk, eggs, and grog with the rest of the cash."

Bex looked at Larceny.

"And the remainder is payin' for your laundry."

"*My* money?"

"We used it all. And our own, too. You gonna gripe about it?"

Bex leapt up from the floor and stood glaring down at Larceny with her hands on her hips. Larceny shook her head. The burst of adrenaline fired by her rage had left her feeling weak and ill. She was helpless and she knew it. This crew had taken her in and were looking after her. How could she begrudge them using her money?

Well, the job with Stella would be no-go now. Anyway, she didn't want to go back because Nick would be able to track her down.

Lynx was unpacking the bags and ramming stuff into the fridge.

"This can go on the bench," he said, hauling out a wine cask.

Larceny flinched, recalling Emma in the Mall and what wine and Avil had done to her.

Lynx threw the empty bags in a corner. He juggled three oranges in his hands.

"Want one?" he said to Larceny.

She shook her head. Right now the thought of food made her feel queasy. She was often like this after a rage attack—stomach churning, weak in the knees. Maybe she should be on antidepressants all the time. No. She wanted to be straight and drug-free. Taking that stuff still made her feel like shit. Woozy shit.

"There's cold pies here, and some snot blocks, a bit squashed, but who's caring?" said Lynx. He brought a pie and a vanilla slice over to Larceny.

"No thanks. I'm not hungry."

"Not good enough for ya, then?" snapped Bex, who was lying on the double bed wolfing down a cold pie. Then catching Larceny's gaze, she dumped the pie on the floor and seized hold of Comma, pulling her onto the bed. She started groping and touching Comma up. Larceny tore her eyes away. It was disgusting. It was gross. She looked back.

Bex peered at her over Comma's shoulder and moved her tongue suggestively. Larceny felt like spewing, although she realized that Bex was putting on a show just for her benefit. She tore her gaze away again and flicked her eyes across to Frantik.

He'd dumped her laundry on the floor near the sofa and was pacing up and down, up and down near the cupboards. Larceny knew the signs. He was hanging out for a taste of whatever he was coming down from. He realized she was watching him, pulled out a packet of cigarettes, lit one up, and took short, angry puffs.

Comma suddenly pulled out of Bex's mauling session. Maybe she'd realized that she was being used to get back at Larceny in some way. She got off the double bed, straightening her clothes. She walked over and sat down on the edge of the sofa.

"Comma. Get back here," Bex commanded.

Comma ignored her.

"You feelin' better?" she asked.

"No."

"Leave her, the bad-tempered bitch. I said come back here," barked Bex. Comma sighed, stood up, and walked over to Bex, who'd got off the bed and plonked herself at the table.

"This is great," said Lynx, switching on the light. He gazed with satisfaction round the small crowded room. To Larceny's world-weary eyes it looked crappy. Tattered curtains flapped at the window. A broken pane let in the cold wintry breeze. The walls were grimy, and newspapers and old cartons littered the floor. The whole place stank of stale tobacco, dope, and alcohol, with vague undertones of urine, decayed food, and dampness. But it was a roof over her head, and she should be grateful.

She wasn't. She resented their help, their intrusion into her life when she wanted to be left alone. She used people for her own ends, so why this feeling of unrest? Was it because she now owed them something? That was crap. Larceny Leyton never owed anybody anything!

Lynx had bought a six-pack and a bottle of Jim Beam. They cracked open the Jimmie and passed it round. She shook her head when Frantik waved it at her.

"Nah."

"Good, all the more for us," said Bex, ripping a tab off a can and glugging down the beer almost in one swallow.

Their talk ebbed and flowed round her as she snuggled back under the blanket. The night spent at Flinders Street Station had left her stiff and sore, and the killing of Sammy Soul—shit. It all came rushing back, the look on his face as she'd swung the bag, the sound his head had made when it had hit the door. The blood . . . oh, *shit!*

She forced herself to think about something else. Often when she felt frazzled and alone she retreated into her own dream world. Her mother rocking her, crooning to her. In her imagination her mother was a beautiful, serene woman with a calm face like the statue of Mary she'd seen in churches. She hadn't really killed herself. It was all a rumor. She was really waiting for Larceny to find her. They'd be together at last and do lovely mother-daughter stuff, like go shopping for clothes and bake cakes and do all the things that TV mothers did with their daughters . . . Her eyelids drooped.

"She's asleep again, the stupid bitch," said Bex.

"Leave her be," said Lynx, his voice tight and angry. For some reason he felt protective toward Larceny. There was a lost and lonely sadness beneath the hard exterior: He recognized and acknowledged it because in a way it was a reflection of himself.

When Larceny woke she was hungry. The room was dark. As her eyes grew accustomed to the gloom she saw that the room was empty. The crew had gone off and left her. Good. She could grab her clothes and get out. She sat up and her head spun.

"You okay?"

The room wasn't empty. A pile of bedclothes heaved on the double bed, and Comma sat up.

"Yeah."

"I'll make you some soup."

"Don't trouble yourself," said Larceny shortly, but Comma had leapt up, switched on the light, and was rummaging in the cupboard.

"Where's everyone?"

"Frantik had to score, and Lynx and Bex have gone cruising. They'll be back soon."

"Bex left you alone with me?"

"She didn't want to, but Lynx said you weren't gay or bi, so she went. Well, he made her go. She knows this area. She's got the best contacts for . . . never mind."

"Dope? Speed? Smack?"

"I didn't say nothin'!"

Larceny dropped the subject. It wasn't important. But how had Lynx known she wasn't gay or bi? Larceny gazed curiously at Comma as she scuttled round in her oversized T-shirt, thick white legs moving clumsily as she found a saucepan and started pouring soup from a can into it.

"I'll toast some of this bread," she said, switching on the griller. It would've been easier to plug in the toaster, thought Larceny, but she didn't say anything.

The soup bubbled over the pan, and the toast started to burn. Comma scraped it busily into the sink, put it onto a plate, slapped wads of margarine onto it, and poured what remained of the soup into a chipped mug. Then she put it on the table. Obviously, she was expected to get up, thought Larceny, peeling back the bedclothes and putting her feet gingerly onto the floor.

"Here."

Comma brought over an armful of clothes—her top, jeans, socks, and undies. With her back to Comma, Larceny put on the clean clothes, pulling her sweatshirt over her head. "I need to go to the toilet," she said.

"We gave you a bucket before. You can't remember?"

"I peed in front of everyone?"

Larceny was appalled.

"Just in front of me. And Bex. The boys turned their backs."

Larceny felt her cheeks burn. They would've heard!

"The bathroom's down the end of the hall," said Comma. "Here's some paper. Don't take long. Your soup will get cold."

Larceny grabbed a towel and the paper and went slowly out into the dark passage. The whole place stank of stale unwashed bodies and the grime of years. She reached the door at the end of the hallway and switched on the light.

The toilet was filthy. She gagged and held her nose as she squatted, not game enough to sit on the seat. She tried not to look at the dirty washbasin when she rinsed her hands. When she turned on the tap only a dribble of rusty water came out. Peering into the shower recess she recoiled at the mold growing on the walls and floor. She decided not to have a shower. She wet a corner of the towel and a knob of soap she found on a ledge, then rubbed the towel over herself, drying off with the rest of it. Later she'd boil up some water back in the room and have a good wash. Although she shouldn't be dirty: She'd had a shower at Nick's that morning. What time was it?

She peered at her watch. Nearly midnight. It felt like a thousand years ago that she'd been eating pancakes at Nick's table.

Where the hell was she?

Standing on tiptoe she peered out of the grimy window. She could see even through the darkness that the building was old and crumbling. It had probably been a hotel in its past life: Now it looked like it should be condemned. Rusty gutters sagged from the roof, and the windows of other rooms she could see from the bathroom were rotten, some with boards instead of glass. She figured by looking down that it was two-storied, which meant she was on the top story.

It had to be somewhere in St. Kilda near the beach, because she could vaguely remember walking through the rain supported by Frantik on one side and Lynx on the other. She wondered where Sal and Lisa, the occupants of their room, had gone on such a cold, wet, miserable day and night.

Walking back along the passage she could hear sounds of occupancy behind the thin walls. Someone snored, someone else groaned as if in pain, and a child whimpered. It was a dump. But then it suited her: She was dump material.

six

LARCENY found the room she'd been in by following the smell of burned toast. The door was still open. She went in.

"Leave the door open," said Comma. "This place stinks of burned toast."

Smoke swirled through the room, but at least it overpowered the other stale, musty smells. She didn't feel like arguing just then, so she left the door ajar.

Comma was still sitting at the table in her oversized T-shirt, staring vacantly at an ad on the TV. Larceny pulled out the other chair and sat down opposite her. The mug of soup was by now half-cold, and so was the toast. Blobs of margarine had coagulated on it, but the toast tasted okay when it was washed down with the lukewarm tomato soup. Comma turned to watch her eat: Maybe it was more fascinating than TV, but it was unnerving having someone staring at you while you were chewing and swallowing.

"So what's your story?" asked Larceny, although she didn't really care one way or the other. The stories were always the same—bashed kids, drunken parents, dead parents, the occasional rich spoiled little shit, parents who'd lost the plot, kids who'd lost the plot.

Comma regarded her with sad, doglike eyes.

"My mum died and Dad got married again to this other woman."

"You didn't like her?"

"She didn't like me. I was a drag in her life. She liked partying all the time."

It figured. Comma wasn't exactly ideal stepdaughter material if you wanted an attractive, slim person to play stepmum to, dress up in designer gear, get identical hair-dos and have girlie chats. On the other hand, Larceny had known some stepmums who were jealous of their stepdaughters because they were young and pretty. Pity Comma's dad hadn't picked one of those to marry. There had to be some good ones, but Larceny hadn't met any.

"When did you clear out?"

"When I was fourteen. I hated home, and I hated school."

"Ah!"

Larceny leaned forward.

"Or did school hate you?"

Comma blinked. She'd never really thought about it in that way. Her mind flashed back like a video player on rewind, primary school, teachers who thought she was dumb, a nuisance, an annoyance because each one thought they could be the one to get through and teach her to read. She still couldn't read: She bought the magazines to look at the pictures. She fast-forwarded to secondary school: the detentions for smoking, for being rude to teachers, for failing to hand in assignments. Yeah, when she thought about it she wasn't exactly the most popular kid in school.

"Schools hated me," said Larceny, when Comma didn't answer.

"Why? Couldn't you read either?" Comma blurted out.

"Course I could read. I got bored shitless, that's all, so I gave them major aggro. Schools are stupid. Teachers are stupid. The whole idea of shoving kids in schools is stupid!"

Larceny banged her mug down on the table to emphasize the point.

"But school's somewhere to go, to fill in time," said Comma, shrugging.

"Yeah? I've got better things to do with my time than sit in some dumb school hearing some dumb teacher go on and on."

"Like what things?"

Larceny shrugged.

"Shoplifting, hanging about, sussing out stuff. I like looking at people, you know? Wondering where they come from, what they're doing, if they're happy, that sort of shit. Not that I ever see too many happy ones unless they're off their faces on something. I guess I'm a sort of roving perv."

Larceny smiled, pleased with her analysis of herself. Comma looked down at her mug. She'd never really thought about what she did and why she did it. She just chugged through each day, her main concerns being to get food, shelter, drugs, and have Bex in her life.

"How did you end up with Bex?" Larceny asked through her last mouthful of toast, looking at Comma's dull, deadpan face. She was such a boring babe. Bex was attractive in a tough sort of way. It had to be a case of opposites attracting each other, a large lifeless lump, and a skinny little spitfire.

"End up?" Comma looked puzzled.

"Well—start up. You know, click onto each other."

"I dunno. We just sort of drifted together."

"When did you . . . how did you know you were gay?" Larceny was surprised to hear herself asking these questions. She usually didn't care about other people or their lives. But part of her wondered what it would be like to have sex with a girl. What did they do?

"I dunno. I just didn't like doing it with guys and then I did it with Bex and it's okay."

"How old are you?" asked Larceny.

"Seventeen."

"You don't look seventeen," Laceny blurted out. Then, seeing the annoyed look on Comma's face, she changed tactics. "I mean, you have a young face. How old's Bex?"

"Same as me."

"So what's her story?"

"I dunno. I know she comes from a posh family, and she's got a twin sister."

"I've got the picture. The twin sister's a goody, right?"

"Dunno. She never talks about her family."

"When did you first . . . I mean, if you've only been with Bex, how do you know you're gay?"

"I dunno. Who said I've only been with Bex?"

"You did!"

Comma rolled her eyes, looked at the ceiling, then got up and rinsed out the two mugs at the sink. She turned on the jug, spooned Nescafé into the mugs, added boiling water, stirred vigorously, then brought the mugs to the table. She plonked them down, slopping coffee onto the red laminate. Then she sat down heavily and regarded Larceny thoughtfully.

"You ever had sex with a girl?"

"No." Larceny wriggled in her chair, feeling embarrassed. Somehow Comma had turned the conversation round and now seemed to be very much in control. Larceny didn't like it: She wished she hadn't started this in the first place.

"Have you had sex with anyone?"

"Of course. Heaps of times," lied Larceny, staring into her coffee cup.

"Was it good?"

"Of course. Otherwise, I wouldn't've done it, would I?"

Larceny sipped at her coffee. It was weak, watery, and tasted foul. She debated whether to get up, pour it down the sink, and make another, but she couldn't be bothered. Comma reached behind her into her bag, dragged out a comb, and started tugging it through her lank brown hair. Larceny drew back from the table in disgust.

"Do you have to do your hair all over the table?"

"Huh?" Comma stared at her. Then with a defiant look she put the comb back in her bag and pulled out a magazine. She flipped it open and started flicking through it.

"I thought you said you can't read!"

Comma kept flicking.

"Hey! I want to talk to you!" Larceny's hand shot out and grabbed the magazine. She tossed it onto the floor.

"I said I *want to talk to you!*"

"What about?"

Comma looked nervous. Her power base was shot to shit. Larceny was making the calls.

"Sex. I want to know when you first did it. Was it with a girl or a guy? What was it like?"

Comma's eyes narrowed with a native cunning.

"Why do you want to know?"

"Just tell me!" hissed Larceny, her anger beginning to grow. Why did Comma have to be so thick, stupid, and stubborn? Why couldn't she just have a normal conversation without all the crap?

"Okay. Okay. If it's that important, I'll tell you," said

Comma, pausing to reach back in the bag for her cigarettes. She took her time lighting up. Larceny drummed her fingers impatiently on the table. Getting information about Comma's sex life was hard work.

"My first time—I was twelve, and this guy talked me into it, you know. He was fifteen. He kissed me, and he tasted of garlic. Yuk. Then we had sex. We did it in a concrete pipe in the playground at the Seventh Day Adventist school one Saturday afternoon. All this gravel was sticking into my bum, and it hurt."

"You mean the gravel, or . . . ?"

"Both. I hated it. I wouldn't do it with him again. Nor anybody else, for ages. Then the next time I had sex I was fifteen."

"How old was the guy?"

"I dunno. Sixteen, seventeen. Why do you want to know?"

"Just curious."

"I was on the run, staying on this farm in a hay shed. This guy Dean lived on the neighboring farm. Anyway, he found me there, and I was scared. But he brought me food and a blanket, so I did it with him."

"Go on. What was it like?"

"I dunno. Just—this guy sweatin' all over me and rammin' into me. That hay, though, it was friggin' prickly."

Comma looked thoughtfully into her coffee cup.

"Go on."

"Then when I was sixteen I tried it with a few guys in the back of cars and stuff, but . . ." she shrugged.

"The earth didn't move for you," said Larceny dryly.

"Huh?"

"Never mind. So Bex is your first partner whom you've *liked* having sex with?"

"I guess so. Last year I met this girl at a party, and we both got drunk. We slept together on the floor. She wanted to kiss me, but I just rolled over on my side and pretended I was asleep when she tried to feel me up. I didn't really fancy her. But I like Bex."

"But do you like sex with Bex?" asked Larceny, her patience beginning to fray at the edges.

"Yeah."

"But how do you know if you're really gay if you haven't had real good sex with a guy?"

"I know I'm gay. I'd rather be with Bex than any guy."

"What about me? Could you fancy me?"

Comma looked puzzled. "You want to do it with me?"

"No," said Larceny, exasperated, "I'm just asking if you could fancy me. I'm trying to find out if you're gay, bi, or confused."

Bex burst into the room.

"I heard that," she snarled. "I knew it was a big mistake to leave Comma with you. You're trouble."

She yanked Larceny's hair almost off her head. "Bitch. Leave her alone."

Larceny drew back her feet and kicked out, hard. She

caught Bex in the chest just as Lynx and Frantik came through the door.

"That's enough!" roared Lynx, pulling Bex off Larceny as she was about to scratch her eyes out. "What's up with you two?"

"She's tryin' to spade Comma!"

"Reality check," sneered Larceny. "I wouldn't touch Comma with a ten-meter pole. No offense meant, Comma."

Comma just gaped stupidly from one girl to the other.

"Come on, Comma, get on some gear. We're goin' out," snapped Bex.

"But—"

"Do it!"

Comma went over to the bed, searched amongst the untidy heap of bedclothes till she found her jeans and top. She dragged her top over her head and pulled on her jeans. Then she turned to face Bex.

"Where're we goin', Bex?"

"Out! Get something on your feet, will ya, and hurry up!"

Comma rummaged under the bed and found her boots. She shoved her feet into them without bothering about socks.

"Why are we—"

"Move it!"

Bex flounced to the door and wrenched it open. Comma followed slowly. Bex grabbed her arm, yanked her through the door, and slammed it shut, hard. There was silence.

"Stay away from Comma," said Lynx, looking at Larceny.

"Oh, man. Don't you start!"

She looked at Frantik for support. He was leaning against the wall with a weird expression on his face. His jacket was saturated, and water dripped from it in a pool round his feet. He put his hand to his throat.

"You okay, man?"

He didn't look too good. His face was chalk white and beaded with sweat. He tried to speak but his tongue seemed too big for his mouth. Larceny frowned. Something wasn't right.

"Look at him, Lynx."

Lynx stared at Frantik.

"What's wrong, mate?"

Frantik mumbled something. Suddenly, Larceny jumped to her feet. She went up close to Frantik and peered at him.

"Have you just scored?" she asked.

"He did," said Lynx. "I turned my back and he was gone. Then he came back looking spacy."

"Did you score from your regular dealer?" said Larceny.

Frantik shook his head and mumbled something.

"You've got a bad whack," said Larceny. "And you're

having something called an anaphylactic reaction. Your throat's swelling up. We have to get you to a hospital."

Frantik looked frantic, shaking his head from side to side, making guttural grunts in his throat.

"No choice, man. You'll die if we don't. Come on."

She looked at Lynx.

"Got any money? We haven't got time for an ambulance. We'll have to get a taxi."

"Yeah," said Lynx, searching his pockets. "I've got about fifteen bucks."

"That'll do it."

Frantik was sagging against the wall, gasping. Together Larceny and Lynx half carried, half dragged him between them down the stairs and into the street. Outside the rain lashed down, and the gutters were overflowing. It was a dirty night to be out. Larceny shivered. She hadn't put on her sneakers, and her feet felt like they were lumps of ice.

"Where the hell's a cab? There's never one when you need it," she said angrily, as the rain plastered her hair flat to her head.

Finally, a taxi slowed, then stopped. Lynx yanked the door open and they pulled Frantik in beside them, falling onto the rear seat in an untidy heap.

"The Alfred," said Larceny to the driver. "Quick."

He was young and cool. He didn't ask questions. He whipped along the streets, tearing through the rainswept night. Luckily he got all the green lights. In what must have been record time he screamed to a halt outside Emergency.

"Thanks, mate." Lynx paid the driver, and they dragged Frantik inside. Larceny raced up to Admissions.

"He's had a bad whack," she gasped.

The woman behind the desk looked blank.

"Bad drugs," Lynx interjected as he supported Frantik, who was clutching at his throat and wheezing for breath. His eyes, the pupils dilated, looked agonized.

"Has he been here before?" asked the woman.

"How the hell would I know?" snapped Larceny. "Get a doctor. Fast."

"Name?"

"Look, lady, he can't breathe," grated Larceny. "Do something!"

She peered over the counter at Frantik, decided it was an emergency, and called a doctor.

"Maybe he needs Narcan," said the young intern who came cruising out to look at Frantik.

"And maybe he needs the antidote to whatever's been pumped into his veins," snapped Larceny. "It's not a heroin OD, it's a bad hit. Adulterated speed. You know, amphetamines."

Then another doctor arrived. He was older and seemed to understand what was going on with Frantik. He got things moving at last. Frantik was wheeled away into a cubicle. Just as well, as he was choking and turning blue.

"Let's get outta here," said Larceny. "Hospitals give me the creeps."

"Wait a minute—shouldn't we hang about? Frantik might need us," Lynx argued.

"What for?"

Larceny was striding for the door, her long hair whipping round her shoulders. Lynx hesitated, then followed her out into the street.

"How do you know all that stuff?" he asked when he caught up to her. "I've been on the street and seen bad whacks, but nothing like that."

"Yeah, well . . . I know anaphylactic reactions because I've had one," said Larceny shortly. "Not from speed. From prescribed drugs when I was in the hospital. And I've seen someone go completely numb from bad speed. Now, shut up and keep walking."

"Will that woman call the cops?"

"Dunno. Maybe. I can't risk it. That's why I'm outta here."

"I'm with you," said Lynx.

They walked quickly away from the hospital and round the corner into St. Kilda Road. Neither of them spoke in their hurry to put some distance behind themselves and the Alfred Hospital.

"I feel bad about leaving Frantik," Lynx finally said when they were several blocks away, still walking fast. "He's my mate. But I don't need cop trouble. I'm on a good behavior bond."

"Yeah? What for?"

"Stealing a car. My old man paid big bail to get me off, but I've got to stay clean or I'll get sent down. Why don't you want to get tangled with the cops?"

She faced him under a streetlight, her large green eyes glowing like a cat's in her white face.

"I killed a guy."

"What?"

She shrugged.

"I killed a guy. Do you want to make something of it?"

The tones were angry, challenging.

"What happened?"

"He was gonna double-cross me, so I killed him. Come on, my feet are freezing." She took off fast across the road, dodging the traffic and narrowly missing getting run over several times. Lynx darted after her.

"Wait up, will ya?"

But Larceny kept striding. She broke into a half trot and then a jog. Lynx pounded alongside her.

"Hey," he puffed. "Slow down, will ya?"

Larceny went faster, as if by running like the devil she could rid herself of her own devils, the ones that rode in her head. But though she ran and ran till her lungs felt as if they would burst, she couldn't run away from the one thing that terrified her the most: herself.

seven

WHEN they got back Bex and Comma were asleep in the double bed. Larceny turned her back on Lynx and stripped off her wet things, leaving them on the floor. She'd sort them out in the morning. She pulled out a clean T-shirt from the pile of laundry and lay down on the sofa, pulling the blanket up to her chin. Lynx pulled the mattress over beside the sofa. He'd also stripped off his wet gear and found a blanket.

"Larce?"

"What?"

"You've got funny feet."

Larceny looked down at her toes. The little toes on both feet were bigger than their companions and curled over. She was the only person she'd ever met who had these weird toes.

"So?"

"Nothin'. Um . . . do you feel like some company?"

"No."

"We'd be warmer if we shared this mattress."

"I'm warm enough."

"I'm not."

She heard him move toward her on his hands and knees. She lay rigid beneath the blanket. She'd kill him if he touched her. The gray mist came swirling, swirling . . . The sofa sagged as he sat down beside her.

"Larce? You're beautiful."

"Piss off," she hissed between clenched teeth.

"I thought you liked me."

"Yeah? Well, you thought wrong."

The rage took over. She jackknifed upright, pushing him hard in the chest. He fell off the sofa onto the floor.

"Do I have to spell it out? *Leave me alone!*"

"All right, all right, don't get so shitty."

He crawled back onto his mattress. After a while his gentle snores told her that he was asleep. But she couldn't sleep. She lay staring into the darkness, her stomach in knots at the thought of him holding her, touching her. He was a nice guy. Why couldn't she unfreeze enough to let him have sex with her? Was there something seriously abnormally wrong with her? All those bloody shrinks hadn't been able to help. . . .

"Why did you feel the need to burn the school down?" one had asked when she was in therapy.

How the hell did she know? The teachers had been on her case for smoking. They'd got in some woman from Quit Smoking to run a course to get her and some of the other girls to quit. But she didn't want to quit, that was the whole point. Who cared if her lungs were full of cancer in twenty years' time? She'd been so angry that they'd imposed their school rules on her she'd gathered dry grass near the school fence and set it alight with her cigarette lighter. She hadn't been burning the school down, just the bloody fence, for shit's sake.

"Why are you so angry? Why don't you like yourself?" another shrink had asked her, staring at her through his thick glasses like she was an alien species from another planet.

"I do like myself," she'd spat at him. "Do you?"

"Like you, or myself?" he'd replied smoothly. She'd felt like smashing his glasses into his face. Smug little prick.

"Oh, who cares? Go to hell," she'd said, turning her back and refusing to answer any more of his dumb questions.

"Uncooperative," she'd seen written on her card. Yeah, well. The few times she'd tried to cooperate it had been the pits. As soon as she'd revealed a weakness the shrink had gone for her jugular. To reveal that you were weak, scared, confused gave them power. And once they had power they could manipulate you, control you. It was all *shit!* Who the hell did they think they were anyway, trying to pry into her soul: God?

Finally, she slept and was woken by Bex crashing

through on her way to the bathroom. She was thirsty and decided to make herself a cup of coffee.

Getting out of bed, she padded over to the sink and put enough water in the jug for one coffee. She spooned Nescafé into a mug and found some milk. She was sitting sipping it when Bex came back.

"Where's the rest of the hot water?" Bex accused, lifting the jug. "That'd be right. Only make enough for yourself. You wouldn't think that anyone else would want a coffee, would you? And where's Frantik?"

"No, I don't ever think of anyone except myself, and Frantik could be anywhere," snapped Larceny.

"What did you do with him last night?"

Bex stood, hands on hips, glaring. Her face was pinched, ugly, and tight.

"We left him at Emergency," said Larceny shortly.

"You left him?"

Bex looked incredulous. Then she narrowed her eyes. "You bitch. Lynx would never leave Frantik on his own. They're buddies, best mates. It was you. You couldn't be bothered staying, could you? You just walked off, didn't you? And Lynx was torn between pissing you off and Frantik in the hospital, and he chose to go with you!"

"Get this," said Larceny. "Lynx walked outta there of his own free will. I didn't ask him to come with me."

"You . . ."

Bex lunged. Larceny picked up the coffee mug and

threw it at her. The hot coffee splashed on her arms and bare feet. She gave a howl and fell back against the sink.

"What the hell . . ."

Lynx rolled off the mattress wearing only his jocks. His eyes went from one girl to the other. Larceny looked at him. Then out of the corner of her eye she saw a movement from the double bed. Comma had woken up and was rubbing the sleep out of her eyes. She was trying to get her brain into gear. She was definitely *not* a morning person, thought Larceny, though it was probably nearer lunchtime. She turned back to Bex who was trying to wipe coffee off her arms. The mug lay shattered at her feet where it had ricocheted off the cupboard onto the floor.

"I've had a gutful of you," said Larceny calmly to Bex. "You're a twisted bitch, and I don't need to be near your space. I'm outta here."

She walked over to her clothes and dragged on clean underwear, jeans, and a top. She found her sneakers and jammed them on her feet. Then she picked up her wet things and stuffed them into a plastic bag.

"You're bad," sobbed Comma, who was comforting Bex.

"Bad and mad, that's me," said Larceny, "and don't you forget it."

She scooped up her tote bag, jacket, and the plastic bag full of wet clothing and sauntered toward the door.

"Wait!"

Lynx had put on his jeans and T-shirt. He pulled on his black Gurus top, and some socks, shoved his feet into his boots, and reached for his jacket.

"Where are you goin'?" wailed Comma frantically.

"With her."

"I don't need no minder, man."

"Yeah? That's what you think."

He followed behind her, slamming the door. Larceny was striding down the stairs.

"Wait up!"

She kept walking.

"Wait!"

She turned and faced him at the bottom of the stairs.

"Why?"

Lynx sighed.

"I dunno. Thought I might come with you."

"You thought wrong."

"Thought you might like a nice hot bath and something to eat."

"Yeah? What are you offering, a room at the Hilton?" she said sarcastically.

"We could go to my place."

"Your place?" Larceny stared at him incredulously.

"My folk's place in Toorak."

"Oh, sure. Your mother's a schoolteacher and they have a place in Toorak?"

"They're rich," Lynx explained patiently. "Old money. I told you, she teaches because she's got to be good at something she sees as useful. And my old man's a dentist. There's big money in teeth."

"I don't get it. You could be home in the comfort, warmth, and safety of your own family room watching TV, and you choose to hang about with lowlife like Comma and Bex? And me?"

"You're not lowlife, Larce. You're just confused."

"Yeah. Right."

Suddenly, Larceny felt tired. Bone-weary. A hot bath would be nice. She shrugged.

"What about your folks?"

"At work. Come on . . ."

It was a long walk through the sleeting rain, along St. Kilda Road, up Toorak Road, and down a side street. It was old money all right: big, stately homes brooding between new money—high-rise apartments with high price tags. Huge trees dripped forlornly, and it was very quiet.

"In here."

Lynx stopped outside a big two-storied brick house with mammoth trees, high walls, and security gates that made Pentridge Prison look like an escapee's paradise. He punched some numbers into a security system built into the side of one of the brick pillars, and the gates swung open.

Larceny hesitated. She didn't like being behind high walls and security gates. It gave her a feeling of insecurity: What if she couldn't get out?

"Come on!"

Lynx was waiting impatiently inside the gates. Once she was inside he went to close them.

"No!" Larceny panicked. "Can you leave them open?"

"The neighbors'll see." Then seeing her tension he relented. "Okay, I'll just pull them together. I won't activate the locks."

They walked up the driveway.

"Keep to the side, then the security camera won't activate the alarm," he said casually when they reached the door.

"Oh, shit. I hate alarms." Larceny froze.

"It's cool. I've got a key. I'll turn it off."

He opened the front door, walked inside, and deactivated the alarm system.

"Come in. It's okay now."

The place made Nick Farino's apartment look like a shit-box. It was very big. And very old. Larceny stood dripping all over a lovely carpet with red, blue, and green swirls all over it.

"Nice rug!"

"It's Persian. I'll show you where the bathroom is. You can take a spa bath while I throw your clothes in the dryer."

Larceny faced him, hands on hips.

"I want to take a bath alone."

"Okay, okay, stay cool. I won't touch you."

"Or perv on me?"

"What do you think I am?" Lynx was quite indignant.

"You are my guest! The bathroom's up the stairs, on the right. Or there's another one farther down the hall, if you prefer that. I'll get you a bathrobe."

Here in his own surroundings Lynx was a different person. He was now the rich kid from the privileged family, private school, education, all manners and charm. Larceny didn't like it. She preferred Lynx the street kid, not Marcus J. Manchester, rich snot. In this place, surrounded by the trappings of the wealthy, she felt like a useless piece of shit. Still, it wouldn't hurt to take a bath, eat some food, hang about for a while. Then she'd bail and get back where she belonged, on the streets.

She went up the wide staircase, along a passage, and found the bathroom. It was huge and had been modernized, with a sunken spa bath, mirrors, fluffy white towels on heated rails, and luxuriant potted plants hanging from the ceiling.

"Wow!"

Larceny turned on the taps and sat on the edge of the tub watching the water swirl into its marbled depths. There were some bath salts in a glass jar on a shelf, so she tossed in a handful. The water turned green, and there was a fresh, pine smell. Through the steam it looked like a churning river pool below a waterfall. Suddenly, there was a knock on the door. She tensed.

"Yes?"

"Toss out your wet clothes."

"Okay."

She peeled them off in a hurry, then wrapped herself in one of the towels. Padding to the door, she opened it.

"Here."

Lynx took them and passed her a thick white toweling robe.

"Enjoy," he said.

Larceny shut the door and leaned against it for a moment, staring through the steam at the bath. She had to trust him, and she never trusted anyone. Could she really trust him? She saw a heavy silver hand mirror lying on the shelf and picked it up. If he came near her, she'd hit him with it. She laid it on the edge of the bath. The tub was nearly full. Leaning over, she turned off the taps and tested the water with one toe. Just right. She dropped the towel and went to climb in. There was another knock at the door.

"Shit!"

She grabbed the robe, put it on, and, holding the mirror like a club, walked over and opened the door.

"What?"

Lynx was standing there with a silver tray on which sat a glass containing a bubbling liquid and some slivers of biscuity-looking stuff.

"Champagne and almond bread," he said, passing her the tray. "A snack while you have a bath."

"Thanks."

She took the tray with one hand and shut the door. Well, this was something new. She'd never drunk champagne and eaten almond bread while taking a spa bath. Okay, so she'd never drunk champagne. Eaten almond bread. Or taken a spa bath. She put the tray on the floor near the bath, took off the robe, and climbed in. The bubbles caressed her like a lovely warm hug that didn't compromise her in any way. Reaching over, she lifted up the glass and took a big swig. The bubbles made her sneeze. It tasted good. Warmth flooded through her, and she giggled. This was better than wine or beer. Nibbling on a piece of almond bread, she settled back in the tub, her thoughts wandering all over the place.

It was crazy. If she had a home like this, she'd be in heaven. Two doting parents, all this wealth and luxury. Lynx had to be a full-on nut to abandon all this and get psychotic about being a Fijian Indian. Who cared if he was dark brown and from another culture?

He cared, that was his problem.

Mentally she went through the list of foster homes she'd had. Maybe if she'd had a rich family from the start, she'd have turned out normal. She'd been fostered out when she was a baby, a nice family in a small country town. Vaguely she could remember being cuddled on her foster mum's lap, read to, rocked to sleep. And her foster dad tickling her and playing this game where he'd toss her into the air and pretend to drop her. But he always caught her. She trusted him. And her foster mum. But then they'd let her down. Dropped her. They had to go to the USA, and they didn't take her with them. At the time she'd felt unwanted, hurt, and abandoned, too young to understand why her foster family dumped her like an unwanted dog. She learned much later that her dad couldn't be found to sign the papers to let them take her, or wouldn't sign them, she wasn't sure. But the emotional damage had been done.

She was put back into residential care and then with another foster family. They'd been very strict because she was hard to control, ripping things up, throwing things, and behaving like a monster because she didn't want to like them or them to like her. There were no guarantees that if she was lovable, they'd keep her. Her first family hadn't, had they? She'd become a biter, had bitten everyone who came near her, bitten all the other kids at the kindergarten. They couldn't handle her. Back into a residential home. Fostered again, too hard to handle, they'd said, back into a home. Back and forth, back and forth like a boomerang, getting angrier, more untrusting, more violent, more feral like an unwanted animal.

Another knock on the door.

"What now?" she yelled.

"You've been in there for an hour. I thought you might've drowned or something."

The water was cold and she hadn't even noticed. She was all wrinkled like a prune and goose-bumpy.

"Okay, I'll be out in a minute."

She pulled out the plug and climbed out quickly. She'd always hated staying in a bath while the water was draining out. When she'd been little she'd been frightened she'd go down the drain with the water. *Old fears hold fast and won't let go,* she thought, jumping in the shower and turning it to HOT to unfreeze herself. Then, wrapping herself in the robe, she scooped up the tray with its empty glass and went back along the hallway and silently down the stairs, the carpet thick and luxurious under her bare feet. Following the sound of music, she found Lynx in the family room.

"What's the group?" she said sourly, standing in the doorway. She knew it wasn't a group as such: It was some orchestra playing the classics.

"London Philharmonic. Some Beethoven. Do you like it?"

"No. It's . . . morbid!"

Lynx shrugged. He was wearing clean blue jeans and a dark blue polo-neck sweater in some soft sort of wool that clung expensively to him. He looked rich, sure of himself, and alien.

"You look like a square," said Larceny in a frosty voice. This new Lynx terrified her.

"Maybe I am."

"You are in this house!"

"That's why I want out."

It suddenly made sense. He looked the part, he played the part, but he felt like an alien in his own environment. Two aliens against the world.

"Here. I've done a couple of TV dinners. I can't cook."

He'd put them on china plates with knives and forks.

"What are they?"

"I dunno. Lean Cuisine shit. I did doubles. I think there's Beef Satay and Chicken Marengo, and I gave us both. Is it okay?"

His voice sounded uncertain.

"Looks great to me."

Larceny sat down, picked up a plate, and began forking up the food. It was hot and tasty.

"Do you want dessert? There's Sara Lee cheesecake or some pecan pie."

"I didn't know rich people ate Sara Lee."

"Get over it, Larce. Rich people eat, sleep, and shit, same as everyone else."

He sounded annoyed.

"Sorry. This is the first time—well—I'll have the cheesecake, thanks."

"And coffee?"

"Yeah. That'd be nice."

He went out of the room with the empty plates, giving Larceny a chance to look at her surroundings. The room was big, with heavy old-fashioned furniture. There was a piano in one corner and a TV built into a console along one wall. Everything was olive green and dark brown: It was a drab, uninviting room, richly furnished with expensive things but unemotional, devoid of any family memorabilia, magazines, or the usual paraphernalia that makes a house a home. It was filled with creature comforts but not comfortable. Little wonder Lynx felt pressured and confined, programmed to be something he wasn't born to be.

The music was grating on Larceny's nerves, so she got up, switched it off, and turned on the TV. It was some dumb program about cross-dressers and the women who loved them. Larceny stared at the screen. Was anyone normal? What was normal?

Lynx came back with a tray. There were two servings of cheesecake and two mugs of coffee. He put it down on the low table.

"Help yourself."

"Thanks."

They ate in silence, both wary of each other. The TV was a lifesaver, an excuse not to communicate as they sat eating the cheesecake and sipping the coffee. Larceny reached in her bag for her cigarettes.

"Sorry. You can't smoke in here," said Lynx apologetically. "No smoking in this house. But I've got something else you might like."

He disappeared, then came back with a plastic bag. He pulled out some syringes, vials of sterile water, and a spoon, along with two capsules.

"Speed?"

"No. Some really good smack."

"I don't do drugs."

"No?"

He seemed surprised.

"This is top H. It'll mellow you out."

"No."

"Okay, okay."

He prepared the fix. Larceny watched TV. It was nothing new to her: She'd seen countless fixes being prepared, watched countless kids shooting up. It neither excited nor repulsed her. As far as she was concerned it was a fact of life. Lynx found a vein, tapped it vigorously with two fingers, then injected.

"Sure you don't want a taste?"

"No. Told you, I don't do drugs."

"Why not?"

"I've had enough shit pumped into me to last a lifetime," she replied shortly.

Lynx smiled as he felt the rush.

"This is good, man," he said, beaming.

"Yeah, right."

The drug gave him confidence. He put his hand on her knee. Larceny jumped like she'd been stung and leapt to her feet, eyes blazing.

"Don't!"

"Okay, okay. Relax. We'll just talk."

"Maybe I don't want to talk."

He laid his head back against the sofa and closed his eyes. Larceny regarded him warily.

"Sit down. I promise I won't lay a finger on you," he said gently.

She sat. He didn't say anything. The TV droned on.

For something to do Larceny picked up the newspaper that was folded neatly on the table.

"Don't mess it up. My old man likes it exactly right when he reads it at night."

"I thought people read papers in the morning."

"Dad's too busy pounding round the streets getting fit. Mum's too busy getting ready for work. Paper-reading's done at night in this house."

"The news of the day's stale by then."

"Yeah. Well, they're not that interested in the rest of the world, are they, only themselves."

Larceny carefully opened the paper, scanning the pages.

"Bid to halt youth suicides," she read out. "What a load of crap!"

"What's it say?" asked Lynx in a slightly slurred voice.

" 'Victoria will supply an extra 550 beds for the mentally ill and set up suicide prevention schemes for young people, the Minister for Health said yesterday. In his first major statement since taking over the portfolio, the minister detailed how the government would spend more than $80 million it has committed to mental health services,' " Larceny read out. " 'The extra money includes a boost to child and adolescent mental services aimed at reducing youth suicide in metropolitan and rural areas. The Health Department would set up suicide prevention networks, and appoint regional suicide prevention liaison officers. Up to 15 percent of young people suffer from psychiatric disorders, but only a small number are diagnosed and treated.' " She stabbed at the article with one finger.

"They haven't got a clue. Typical government. Why don't they try to stop kids from getting suicidal in the first place? Why don't they look at the reasons? It's just a load of bullshit, spending money to make themselves look good!"

"How do they know there's 15 percent of basket cases if only a small number are diagnosed?" said Lynx, opening his eyes. "From the kids I've seen there's more likely 40 percent."

"Meaning?" Larceny glared at him.

"Meaning I've seen heaps of real screwed-up kids. More than 15 percent."

"Meaning me?"

"Yeah. You."

He said it matter-of-factly. Larceny sucked in her breath. She felt the familiar rage begin to swell like an oversized bubble in her chest. She threw down the paper angrily.

"And you're not? Sitting there blissing out on H, when you've got all this . . . this . . ."

She waved her arms wildly to encompass the room and all its trappings

"Okay, I'm screwed-up, but I'm not crazy!"

"Why did you kill that guy, then?"

"What?"

Larceny stared at him. She'd forgotten that she'd told him.

"Why did you kill the guy? How? Where? When? What for?"

"It doesn't scare you that I killed someone, that I might kill you?" she grated, glaring at him.

"I don't care if you do. It'd solve all my problems," he said.

"Crap. That's the smack talking. And why should I tell you, anyway? It's none of your business."

He looked at her dreamily. The rush had gone, and he was beautifully mellow, at peace with the world, the euphoria cruising through his whole being, relaxed in his drug-induced paradise.

"To kill or be killed, that is the question," he murmured. "Why did you kill him?"

"He was giving me major grief," she snapped.

"Who?"

"Sammy Soul."

"Good name. Hope his soul's happy. How do you know he's dead?"

"I just know, that's all. Look, I'm sick of you asking me questions like a bloody shrink, I'm sick of all this rich shit. I've had a bath, I've eaten your food, I'm grateful and all that, but I just want to go now, okay?"

"Sure," said Lynx. "You're free to go anytime, babe. Don't let your love for me hold you back."

He giggled.

"You're off your face, man. I'm outta here."

She grabbed up her bag. "Where's my clothes?"

"In the dryer. And don't slam the door on your way out!" He giggled again.

That H was a real mind-spinner. Larceny whirled away, heading for the laundry. She finally found it, yanked the door of the dryer open, and put on her clothes. They were still warm. He hadn't done her jacket or the stuff in the plastic bag. Her eyes lit upon a Dri-as-a-Bone coat hanging on a hook. Probably his old man's. Well, tough. He could afford another one. Dragging it on, she rolled back the sleeves, then stormed back down the passage, the tote bag bumping against the wall. She paused in the family room.

"Hey, man. Fair exchange. My company and a bag of wet clothes for this coat."

She paraded in front of him, but his eyes were closed. Lynx was totally out of it. So, who cared? He was just another chunk of floating flotsam in her life. She went out, banging the door behind her. *Good riddance, goodbye, and best of luck, Lynx. You need it!*

eight

It was pouring. The rain pelted down, running in rivulets off Larceny's coat. She was grateful for its warmth and bulk. She still had a change of underwear in her tote bag. Who needed extra clothes? Something would turn up. It always did. She could shoplift a new wardrobe if she needed new gear. If you had food in your belly and warm, dry clothes, that was a bonus. She marched down the drive, pushed open the gates, and headed off down the street toward Toorak Road.

Lynx was a nice guy, but a loser. Rich, poor, they were all the same, and when it came to the crunch, you were on your own. If he did manage to get himself over to Fiji, he was still going to be a misfit. He was culturally confused in his own head. He was really an individual: his own person. But he had to find that out for himself. And Larceny didn't have the time or inclination to unconfuse Lynx. She had her own life to find, to live. Such as it was.

No money. The crew had used it all. She put her hand in the pocket of the coat and closed it round—money! Two twenties and a ten. And a handful of small change. Laughing, she looked up through the rain into the clouds and beyond.

"Thanks, God," she said. Not that she really thought there was one, but she always seemed to score when things were down. A pessimistic optimist was how one shrink had described her.

Now, what to do with fifty bucks? Get a taxi? Get a room for the night? Go to the movies? She was rich. She was free. No ties, no worries, not a care in the world. She hit Toorak Road and turned toward the city. She'd get a bus. One came trundling up out of the rain, and she sprinted across the road, the tote bag banging against her as she dodged between the crawling cars and swung herself up the step.

The bus was full of schoolkids, private-college types. They looked sideways at her as she threw back the hood, sending a shower of droplets all over anyone who was in a yard radius. She looked at them boldly. Some of the girls dropped their eyes. Several of the guys looked interested. With her shiny red hair and devilish green eyes she radiated a come-hither magnetism that concealed a contemptuous attitude to anything or anyone that reeked of money and prestige. And anything that smacked of institutionalism—schools, hospitals, psych wards, and residential homes. She was free. And they were strangling in a web of conventions and social systems that made them prisoners in mind, body, and soul.

She gazed out the window, wrapped up in her own thoughts, as kids got off the bus, slogging through the rain to their houses, their prisons of respectability. She chuckled. Several people glanced at her and then away, perturbed, because you weren't supposed to sit on a bus laughing at nothing. The bus rounded the corner into St. Kilda Road. Larceny saw the spire of the Cultural Center and on a whim, decided to get off there and explore. Why not?

Jumping down, she walked across the expanse of paved brickwork, past the sculpture that looked like a beached hippopotamus, and through the sliding glass doors. Lush red carpet, polished brass, and mirrors everywhere, and an escalator going down to a lower level. Down below there was an exhibition of costumes worn by opera stars. Larceny stood gazing in wonder at the richly embossed dresses and the plethora of colorful silks and satins. She reached out a tentative hand to stroke one of the dresses.

"Don't touch the exhibits," said a custodian who was standing nearby.

Larceny flicked him a scathing glance.

"Say 'please' and I won't," she said gently, her hand still stroking the fabric.

"Did you hear me? I said don't touch!"

"Please!" Larceny snapped. She put down her bag and deliberately stroked the dress with both hands.

He grabbed at her.

"Don't touch me, *per-lease!*"

She tugged hard, and the delicate fabric of the skirt parted from the bodice. He stood aghast, as with a mocking laugh Larceny whipped up her bag and whirled away toward the stairs.

"He only had to say 'Please,' " she said to a woman who was standing there with a shocked look on her face. "It doesn't cost anything to say 'please,' you know."

"You're crazy," gasped the woman, backing against the wall.

"I know!"

Taking two stairs at a time, Larceny raced up to the street level and darted through the doors. She pulled up her hood again as the driving rain stung her face. Head down, clutching her bag tightly against her, she headed over the bridge toward Flinders Street Station. She glanced back over her shoulder. No one was following her. Pity about the dress: She hadn't meant to tug it so hard. Still, it could be sewn back on again. If he'd only spoken nicely to her, she wouldn't've lost her temper.

She reached the station, a familiar comfort zone, and, squatting against a wall, she lit a cigarette. Smoking was something to do. The nicotine had somehow never become an addiction. She could take it or leave it. She looked round at the food stalls, the hustling, bustling people. Home sweet home. She looked back down at her feet.

"Larce!"

Her head jerked back up again. Now what? Did everyone in this pisshole of a city know her? A familiar foxy face was staring down at her.

"Hi, Jane."

"You owe me," said Jane, standing in front of her, hands on hips. The black rucksack on her back made her look like a snake-necked tortoise.

"Yeah? You and half of Australia." Larceny drew hard on her cigarette and deliberately blew smoke up into the angry face looming down at her.

"You were s'posed to divide the shoplifting money. Cathy and I waited, but you never showed."

"Yeah? Well, I didn't get any money. Sammy Soul pulled a swifty."

"That's what you say."

"Look, I don't need any grief. I killed him, he's dead, there's no money, okay?"

Jane's mouth fell open.

"You killed him? When?"

"When I did the runner. Last week, day before yesterday, I dunno, I can't remember. A lot's happened in the last few days."

"He was alive and well yesterday," said Jane. "I know, because I hocked a gold bracelet. The rat only gave me fifty dollars and it was worth at least two hundred."

Larceny blinked. "Alive? Sammy Soul? He's not . . . I didn't kill him?"

"Yeah. Pity you didn't, but—"

Jane squatted beside her, her thin sly face eager and curious.

"What happened?"

"He was cheating on me, so I walloped him with the bag of stuff. I thought I'd killed him."

"Nah." Jane grimaced. "You didn't even do any major damage, though, come to think of it, he did have a Band-Aid on his forehead."

"Yeah. Right."

So the little slime was alive and well. And she'd been thinking she was a killer. All that agonizing for nothing. Okay, so she hadn't been exactly agonizing, but it was nice to know she wasn't a murderer after all, she wasn't Victoria's Most Wanted. She wasn't anyone's most wanted.

"What are you doing here?" she asked Jane.

"Left. Done a runner."

"What about Cathy?"

"That stupid slut? She's gone to bits since Emma OD'd, can't get any sense outta her."

"Wait. Wait. Emma OD'd? When? Where?"

"In the Mall a few days ago. Accidental, like. Wine and Avil."

"Accidental?"

Larceny recalled Emma's tired, pinched face, the look of the lost, unwanted, unloved, and tormented, and shook her head.

"That kid knew exactly what she was doing," she said softly. "Exactly!"

She felt the anger beginning to boil. The gray mist gathered before her eyes and the voices began their screeching chant. "Hurt. Hurt. Kill."

"Kill who?" she said aloud, holding her screaming head. "I can't kill the whole friggin' government!"

"What?"

She was aware of Jane peering at her. "What are you mumbling about, Larce?"

"Never mind!"

Larceny shook her head, trying to clear away the mists of anger. All that crap in the paper she'd just read back at Lynx's house. Half the suicides they'd put down as "accidentals" to make their stats look good. Now, Frantik was a genuine OD. She smiled grimly. They'd probably put him down on their computers as an attempted suicide. Jesus, would they ever get it right?

"Where're you sleepin', then? Got a spare bed?" asked Jane, with that foxy look on her face again. She was street smart, a real survivor, but definitely not to be trusted at all.

"Plenty of spare beds," said Larceny laconically.

"Great. Where?"

"Here."

"Here?"

"Roof over my head. Food on tap. What more could I want?"

"You live here?"

"And other places," said Larceny shortly, thinking of the one-room filthy flat and Lynx's Toorak mansion.

"I'm gonna find Paul. He said to meet him here, 'cause this is where he hangs. Have you seen him?"

"Nup. Don't want to, either. He's bad news."

"He's got some good deals going on," said Jane.

"Yeah? In his head!"

Jane pulled off the rucksack and squatted beside Larceny.

"He's into some network. Moving stuff, ya know?"

"I thought he was going straight after his last time in court. That's what he told me, although I didn't trust him. He's always too smooth. I thought his mum turned up and was going to reform him."

"Yeah, well, he went to live with her for a while. She told him she'd always wanted him but after her mental breakdown when he was a baby she couldn't cope, see, so she stayed in Queensland and his old man took him and his two brothers down here and brought them up."

"Dragged them down, more like," said Larceny. Paul's old man was a known small-time crim. "So what happened with his mum and going straight?"

"Dunno. She just couldn't control him."

"Yeah? Maybe he's old enough and stupid enough now to control himself." Larceny spat out the words with a sudden surge of viciousness. Paul had a mother, which was more than she did. Larceny had spotted them walking together through the Mall. Paul's mum had looked nice: a little woman with an anxious expression but a kind, gentle face. Controlling Paul would've been hopeless for her. Schools couldn't do it. Cops and courts couldn't do it. Youth Training Centers couldn't do it. Why the hell had she even attempted to do it? She'd been doomed to failure before she even started!

"You sure you haven't seen him round?"

"No."

Jane bit her lip and looked worried. Then she shrugged.

"No sweat. I'll cruise with you for a bit."

"Yeah. Great." Larceny's voice was heavy with sarcasm, but it was wasted on Jane, who'd dragged out a packet of cigarettes and looked like she was settling in for the duration. "Anyway, seeing as you're here, tell me about Cathy. Why did she go to pieces about Emma?"

"Didn't you know? They're half sisters. Same father, different mothers or something."

"Yeah? Well, she didn't worry too much about Emma when she was alive," said Larceny. "If that had been my half sister, I'd have . . ."

Then she stopped. Her half sister? She had found it hard not to hurt her own two stepsisters. What was she thinking? Living in this city was softening her brain.

"It's getting colder," said Jane, shivering. "Are you sure you wanna sleep the night here?"

"Dunno. What have you got in mind, rooms at the Park Royal or something?"

"It's my first time here. I thought . . ." Jane's voice trailed away, and she looked scared. For such a street-smart kid she wasn't doing a great job of controlling herself. She'd always run with a pack and liked showing off to the crew. Alone she was just a marshmallow. But then lots of so-called tough kids were. Larceny inwardly groaned. She didn't want to be stuck with Jane. Or anyone else. Life was hard enough without hangers-on dragging along. Unless of course . . .

"Wanna do a couple of shops?" she asked. She might as well make use of Jane if she was going to hang about.

"Yeah, well, I . . ."

"Well, if it isn't Miss Bitch," said a familiar, hard voice.

Larceny looked up. It was Bex, looking tough, rough, and unforgiving.

"Glad to see you, too," she said.

"This is our patch. Get lost," said Bex.

"Yeah?"

Larceny got to her feet. This cow bitch wasn't going to tell her to get lost.

"Hi, Larce."

It was Comma, clutching a swag of magazines, with Frantik close on her heels. He still looked kind of spacey. He had the shakes, bad.

"Hey, man. You okay?"

"No thanks to you," hissed Bex. She looked at Jane. "She left him in the hospital, just walked out on him."

"Aw, grow a brain, Bex," said Larceny. "Lynx and I couldn't do anything, could we? What did you expect us to do, sit and hold his hand?"

"I was fine," said Frantik, his hands twitching. "They pumped some shit into me and put me under observation, but I split when I got the chance. Larce is right. She and Lynx couldn't have done anything. Where is he, by the way?" His eyes darted about, searching.

"Home on an H trip," said Larceny shortly. "And how come you guys are here, anyway? I thought you had it all together, place to stay, all the comforts of home."

"Yeah, well Sal and Lisa came back," said Comma as Jane stood up. "Who's this?"

"Jane. This is Comma, Bex, and Frantik," said Larceny. "The Melbourne crew. They run this place. They run Flinders Street Station. They think."

Bex glared and clenched her fists. Larceny smiled nicely at her, just to wind her up.

"I'm looking for a guy called Paul," said Jane. "You know him?"

"Nah. Never heard of him," replied Bex shortly, jamming her hands in her pockets. She knew she didn't stand a chance: Larceny was taller, stronger, and meaner. And she was a nutter, and therefore unpredictable. It was more face-saving to split. "Come on, we're outta here." She turned and wheeled away.

Jane looked at Larceny. "Are we going, too?"

"Suit yourself. I'm not."

Jane looked undecided as Comma shrugged and followed Bex. Frantik ambled after them, shaking his head from side to side as if to clear it from whatever drug-demons were dancing in his brain.

"Wait for me!" Jane grabbed her rucksack and ran after Frantik. Larceny smiled. Alone again. That's what she preferred. She sat back down against the wall on her haunches and gazed at the passing crowd. She'd do some people-watching to fill in the time, then she'd buy something to eat, maybe drop in on Stella's hot-food van. Might do some work if Stella offered it. She didn't need the money but it was something to do, something to fill in the time just as long as Nick Farino didn't try and give her aggro. Nah, she'd given him the flick.

Her mind wandered. Sammy Soul was still alive. Had he reported her to the cops? No, that was doubtful; Sammy was the type who didn't want cops sniffing about. And Emma. Dead. She'd been quite a nice kid, no trouble, kept to herself, usually dead drunk sleeping it off in the Mall. And Cathy was her half sister?

She hadn't known that. Paul was in Melbourne somewhere. Well, his parole officer wouldn't be too thrilled that he'd done a runner. Paul was a dipstick. Always in trouble. The last time he'd got caught for burglary, he'd got let off with a warning, "Behave yourself or else," and he'd walked straight out of the court into a store and taken a carton of cigarettes. Dumb. It was almost as if he was begging for them to lock him up. He'd got hauled back before the judge and given a good behavior warning. It was a joke. Still, what was the system supposed to do with losers like Paul?

Maybe they shouldn't have let him become a loser in the first place!

All bloody losers. Jane. She'd been in and out of homes since she was six and her parents had split. Cathy, thick as two bricks, a school dropout at the age of eleven. Bex. Comma. Frantik. They'd all lost the plot. And Lynx. He was the dumbest of them all. Good home, rich parents, all he had to do was play ball and go through with the dentist thing, forget about being Indian/Fijian, and he was set up for life. Who needed to cruise with losers?

She didn't. She was the legendary Larceny Leyton. She didn't need anyone. She wasn't a loser, she was a survivor with a high IQ. The government. Society. Everybody—they could all go to hell!

She put her head on her knees and pressed her eyes hard so that the tears wouldn't flow, would stay dammed up inside. Larceny Leyton had no patience with self-pity or tears.

"Hel-lo."

She looked up. A weird sight met her eyes. There was a thin man about sixty gazing at her. He was dressed like a businessman or executive, but somehow it looked all wrong. He was wearing a cream suit with flared trousers, black shirt, green-and-mauve tie, and a brown-felt hat. A long white silk scarf completed his ensemble. An expensive-looking black umbrella with a carved gold handle was nonchalantly being swung from his one hand. He had the most peculiar-looking face, flattened and creaseless like a cardboard overlay, with black beady eyes like currants staring curiously at her. Then he smiled.

"Come and have some tea with me," he said in an odd singsong sort of voice. "There's some seats round the corner. It's not good for you to sit on the cold floor."

"I don't feel like tea, thanks. I've just eaten."

"No, I mean a cup of tea."

"No, thanks."

"Come. I'm sure you will like it."

"No, I don't . . ."

"You will come!"

It was an order, not an invitation. He poked her playfully with the point of his furled umbrella. Short of creating a fuss, there was nothing she could do but pacify him and have the tea. He couldn't attack her in the middle of the station, could he?

Heaving a sigh, she got to her feet. He was nuts, she was sure: She'd seen enough weirdos in psych hospitals to recognize the signs. Probably harmless. Probably lonely. It was easier to have the tea, then bail. Holding her arm he steered her toward the seats. Resisting the urge to pull away, hating to be held, she kept walking beside him.

"There, my dear." He pulled her down onto a bench and waved his hand imperiously at the woman behind the snack bar.

"Tea, please, Mildred."

"Okay, Sir Harold," said the woman with a resigned smile.

So he was known. He must be one of the many wandering characters who had been turfed out of his mental home when the government had closed it down. Another lost and lonely soul.

The woman brought over a tray with two cups and saucers, a silver teapot, a matching milk jug and sugar bowl, and put it down on the seat between them. Her name tag said "Denise."

"There you go, Sir Harold," she said, as if she was serving him in a posh dining room at a table with a crisp white cloth. Larceny gave her a brief smile. The woman was kind. She obviously pandered to this old man's fantasies and a few minutes every day cared for him by serving him and his 'guest.'

"Thank you, Mildred," he said graciously. Then he turned to Larceny.

"I gave her this teapot, milk jug, and sugar bowl," he said. "Family heirlooms. Do you know, she only had these tea bags, and little paper packets of sugar? And she had to pour the milk from a carton. Isn't that dreadful? Did you know I'm really Jesus, the Son of God? I was crucified on the Cross!"

Larceny looked at him.

"Did it hurt?"

He blinked. No one had ever asked him that before. Some people turned away, shocked. Some people tried to bombard him with trick questions. Others in white coats tried to inject him or push pills down his throat. He thought about it. Did it hurt? Did what hurt? He'd already forgotten, his short-circuiting brain leaping across another neurotransmitter to a different topic.

"I was born in a castle," he said, pouring tea into the cups. "I'm from the French nobility. And you, my dear?"

"I was probably born in a cardboard box," said Larceny, grinning at him.

"Oh, very droll, my dear. Very droll." He looked at her quizzically, head on one side like a sparrow. "Milk?"

"Yes, please."

"Good." He leaned forward as he handed her the tea. "I shot President Kennedy!"

"Why?"

He blinked again. No one had ever asked him why, either. He was beginning to enjoy chatting with this young lady. She was very intelligent. He opened his mouth to explain why, but the thought went fleeing out of his head. "Sugar?" he asked politely.

"Thanks."

"You look like Isadora Dalleau, my dear," he said, studying her face intently. "She was married to my friend

Count Hugo Dalleau, you know. The same red hair. The same green eyes."

"Maybe I'm related," said Larceny with a grin. It would be nice to be related to a countess.

He looked at his watch. "My goodness, how the time flies. I'm late for my appointment."

He leaped to his feet, bowing as he kissed her hand, and was gone, melting into the crowd before Larceny had time to collect her thoughts. She stared at the teacup still in her hand, at the silver teapot, milk jug, and sugar bowl. Remnants of his past life or props for the present?

She'd enjoyed his old-world charm. Typical. The one person she'd actually liked had whizzed off. A real crazy. Maybe that's why she'd got on so well with him. Two nuts together. But she wasn't really mad. Just those voices taunting, going on and on . . .

"Thanks, love. He often can't find anyone to chat with him. He's totally batty but quite harmless."

"Huh?"

Denise, alias Mildred, was scooping up the tray. She rushed back to her food stall. It was closing time. The shutters were going down, and the traders were packing up.

Larceny decided to lie down on the bench.

"Don't settle there, love," said Denise, walking past with her overcoat on, obviously heading for home. "That's Solomon's permanent bench."

Larceny wondered whether she should fight someone

called Solomon for bench rights and decided she couldn't be bothered. She went back to her wall space and hunkered down, sitting on her tote bag. It looked like she'd be in for a long, cold night.

nine

"Hi, there."

Shit. What now? Couldn't she be left alone?

Larceny raised her head and groaned. A Salvo. That was all she needed. She put her head back down on her knees again.

"I thought you might like a warm bed for the night," said the Salvo in a kindly voice. Why did religious types always have the same tone of voice like they were doing you a big favor by noticing your existence?

"I'm fine, thanks. I'm waiting for someone," Larceny lied. She looked round. She must've been sitting against the wall for hours. Her legs were cold and stiff, and round her the night flotsam was drifting in and settling down for the evening.

"I'm Kevin," he said, squatting beside her. She shot him a sideways look. Young, earnest, a pink face, wire-rimmed glasses behind which gray eyes regarded her compassionately. "Who are you?"

"Good question."

Who was she? Larceny Leyton, fifteen, nearly sixteen, female, loner, sometimes psycho, as people thought. But she knew better.

"What's your name?"

He was persistent.

"Larceny."

"Larceny? That's an odd—er—what's your last name?"

"Leyton."

"Oh. Well, Larceny Leyton, you look like you could do with a nice hot meal and nice warm bed."

"Why?"

Her question threw him. He frowned.

"You're sitting here alone. You've been here for quite some time."

He'd been watching her. She was about to tell him to get lost when out of the corner of her eye she noticed a guy in a black-leather jacket walking through the far doorway near the clocks. Was it Nick? She wasn't sure, but . . .

"Yeah. Right. I'll take the bed," she said, jumping to her feet. "Let's go."

Kevin was taken aback. Her sudden change of heart had shocked him and thrown him off-balance. He got awkwardly to his feet as she faced him, clutching her tote bag. Then she wheeled away, making for the exit into Swanston Street. He followed, striding to keep up with her. She paused in the street, looking back at him.

"So. Where's the warm bed?"

She waved a hand at the crawling traffic, the driving rain.

"Not far. We can walk."

"You'll get wet!"

She said it with a trace of sarcasm in her voice, and, as if to make her point, pulled up her hood.

"I've got an umbrella."

She hadn't noticed it in his hand. He undid the tab and, opening up the umbrella, raised it high above his head.

"Ready?"

"Sure. Take me to your leader, Kevin."

They walked across with the lights along Flinders Street and down another street to a dark, grim-looking building. A few vagrants were shambling through the entrance, wet and cold, wrapped in their personal misery. Larceny jammed on her brakes.

"Hang on, man. I'm not going in there with them."

"No, the adolescent accommodation is next door. This is where the food is, Larceny."

"I'm not hungry."

She was frightened. To be classified as a vagrant, to line up in a soup kitchen with the lost and lonely, to be a charity case? Forget it.

"It's good food. There's tomato soup, roast chicken, and banana custard."

"I hate tomato soup, chicken, and custard," she snapped.

"Well . . ." Kevin seemed nonplussed. His job was to

rescue the homeless, provide food and shelter, and do God's work. No one had ever complained about the food before. Maybe she was just an ungrateful little street kid who was on the run for kicks. Then he saw the hunted look in her eyes, and realized with shock that she was scared. He capitulated.

"Would you rather have a burger and fries?" he said.

"They make burgers and fries in there?" She jerked her thumb at the doorway.

"No. At Burgermania down the street. I'll treat you."

"No. I'll treat you!" She grinned at him, and it was as if a halogen light had been switched on from the inside. She was radiant! He blinked. She was very beautiful in a wild, untamed sort of way. He saw the intelligent acknowledgment of his surprise gleaming in her eyes and the mocking smile curving her lips. He was so astounded that he caved in straight away.

"Okay. I don't get treated very often."

"I'll just bet you don't."

He had a sudden awful thought that maybe her money wasn't honestly acquired, but wisely bit his tongue as they walked round the corner and down another street toward the welcoming big pink-plastic icon that symbolized Burgermania.

They went inside. It was noisy, warm, and steamy with bodies and food. A few customers looked with surprise at the young Salvo and the wild-looking girl at his side, then went on eating. It was none of their business. Kevin and Larceny walked up to the counter and gave their orders.

"Eat in or take-out?" asked the girl whose picture beamed at them from the wall behind her announcing that she was crew person of the month. Her badge said 'Katie.' *Katie the Crew Person of the Month,* thought Larceny. Was that her fifteen minutes of fame? Andy Warhol had said that everyone on the planet was due fifteen minutes of fame. So where was hers? And when was it coming?

"We'll eat here," said Kevin, as Larceny wondered what you had to do to be crew person of the month. Sell more burgers? Be nice to the customers? Make the most money? Be a team person? But then, who cared? And who wanted to jerk burgers round all day long? Who wanted to be famous anyway?

Katie was quick. That's how she got to be crew person, Larceny decided, as if by magic two burgers, fries, and Cokes appeared on the tray. Rummaging in her pocket, she found a twenty and handed it over. Katie's lightning fingers moved over the till keyboard, then she handed over the change.

"Thanks."

Larceny pocketed the change and picked up her tray. Kevin followed her with his tray to a spare table.

"This is a first," said Larceny, biting into the thick burger, melted cheese dribbling down her chin.

"A first? Burgermania?"

"No. Having a meal with a rep from God. What's it like, being a Salvo?"

"It's exhausting sometimes, but it has its rewards."

"Yeah? Like what?"

"Like rescuing kids off the streets."

"Meaning me?"

She looked at him over the top of her burger.

"You. And others."

"What if I don't want to be rescued? What if I'm too bad to be saved?"

"You are one of God's children," he said seriously.

"One of God's children, eh? So. What's He or She done for me?" She took a sip of her Coke, watching him warily.

Kevin considered this carefully. "You're alive, you're well, you're in a country where there's no wars and oppression, you're . . ."

"Oh, per-*lease.* Spare me the sermon, Kev. My life's a shithole."

"But it needn't be like that. If you put your life in God's care . . ."

Larceny banged her Coke down so hard it slopped all over the table.

"Forget it, man. I don't trust anybody with my life, especially some spirit in the sky who's done absolutely zilch for me so far, except maybe let me find some money in this coat pocket."

"Maybe you haven't given God a chance."

"And maybe God hasn't given me a chance."

She felt the anger bubbling up, the gray mist swirling into her brain. She gripped the cup so hard that it split and the Coke ran in a brown sticky river all over the tabletop.

"I'm outta here."

She jumped up, stuffing the last of her fries into her mouth.

"Wait!"

He was on his feet, coming at her, reaching for her with his hands. No. She couldn't stand being touched, grabbed. NO! She snatched up the umbrella, holding it like a lance, jabbing him back. There was a stunned silence as the diners watched in horror, their forgotten burgers halfway to their lips.

"Larceny, calm down. Look, just sit down quietly, and we'll talk this through."

But the voices were taunting, chanting, screeching in her head.

"Hurt. Hurt. Kill!"

She went for his face with the umbrella, belting him with it, wielding it like a sword. He ducked, trying to cover his head with his hands. She was like a mad thing, hitting, striking out with a demented fury as he backed away. His glasses fell off and crunched under her feet as she lunged again.

"Hey. Stop it!"

A big burly man leaped up from his seat and tried to

grab the umbrella from her. She whirled and kicked out at him. Chairs crashed, people screamed as she lashed out blindly, consumed by a red rage that ripped through her, giving her superhuman strength. Kids started crying, and people cowered in their seats as they watched her assault with astounded eyes.

"What's wrong with her?" cried a woman above the din.

"She's psycho. Probably on drugs," said a man, ducking as Larceny crashed through the melee, swiping wildly with the umbrella. It hit a chair and broke in half.

"That's enough."

The big burly guy grabbed her and pinned her arms behind her back. She struggled, kicked, spat, and swore as two cops came charging through the door. Katie had been superquick on the phone. They must've been practically cruising past the door! Larceny fought and struggled as hands seized her. The cuffs went on. Suddenly, beaten and defeated, she slumped and would have fallen if one of the cops hadn't caught her. All the anger and rage drained out, and she was just a confused, scared kid.

"What the hell happened here?" asked the cop, staring at her bent head and then at the chaos round him.

"She's sick, man. A total psycho," said a young guy in the corner. Kids were still wailing as the cops hustled her through the door and out into the street. Kevin followed, wiping bits of burger from his uniform.

"Do you know this young woman?" asked a cop.

"Yes. Well, I know her name but no personal details. We were having a meal, and she suddenly went berserk."

Larceny looked at him from under her tangled mane of red hair and blinked. Where was she? She twisted her head and looked down at her hands. What was she doing handcuffed? What had happened? Who was this Salvo?

Then it came rushing back. The voices. Telling her to hurt. To kill. Oh, God. Had she killed somebody? Was she really a psycho? She looked at Kevin.

"I'm sorry," she whispered. "I can't control them anymore. When you tried to touch me, I got so scared. Then I heard the voices, and they said, 'Hurt. Kill.' I can't make them stop. When I'm angry I can't."

She started to cry, great gut-wrenching sobs.

"We'd better get her to the hospital," said one of the cops. "She's a real nutcase. On drugs for sure."

They put her in the cop car. Kevin got in beside her and put his arm round her. For once she didn't flinch away. She was too tired, too scared, and too lonely inside.

"I'm here with you," he said. "You'll be all right soon. Tell me, has this happened before?"

Before? thought Larceny dully. A thousand times before. She thought she'd beaten the voices, had them in control. Thought it was the dope she'd chuffed, all the psycho drugs they'd given her over the years that had caused the voices. She hadn't smoked dope for weeks, hadn't taken her antidepressants, knew she could beat the bloody voices in the end, control her rages. And now this!

They arrived at Emergency. And it was the Alfred. It seemed ironic that she was being admitted to the very hospital where she'd brought Frantik when he'd got his bad whack. He'd walked out, but would she be able to do the same? They'd pump her full of sedatives, then send her back to a psycho hospital, more drugs, more shrinks trying to shrink up her brain.

"I'll stay with her," said Kevin, as they took her into a cubicle. "I don't think you need to be here," he said to the cops, as one cautiously undid her handcuffs. *Fool. Idiot,* thought Larceny, looking at the cop underneath her lashes, did he think she was going to attack him? She didn't have the strength left to swat a mosquito. A nurse peeled off her coat and took off her shoes. A doctor arrived, looking harassed. Wet rainy nights in a big city always brought a multitude of accidents. He had a pedestrian with a head injury, a couple of whiplash victims from rear-enders, more road-accident victims with lacerations, suspected broken bones, and internal bruising, a drunk who'd fallen down some stairs, and a kid with second-degree burns from falling onto a heater. There was no room, no beds, and he was tired. He pulled back her sleeve to inject her with a sedative in case she started performing again and saw the scars.

"Shit!"

He seldom swore and was seldom shocked. He'd seen

it all before. But the multiple scars told their own terrible tale. Kevin sucked in his breath, and the two cops looked at each other over Larceny's head.

"Maybe we should stay," said the older one.

"No, she'll be fine. I'll sedate her, and you can talk to her in the morning," said the doctor, noting with professional eyes her waxy pallor and exhausted face. "She needs to sleep. We'll run some blood tests and find out what she's been using."

"Nothing," mumbled Larceny, but her tongue felt too big for her mouth, and she only managed a weak whimper as the needle slid into her arm.

When she woke up it was dark. She was in a hospital ward. Someone was snoring in the corner bed, and there was a faint light from the nurses' station down the hall. Cautiously, she turned her head, expecting to find cops and security glaring down at her, but there was no one. Not even Kevin, God's messenger and willing worker. So much for keeping his word. Larceny's lips curved contemptuously. She'd let down her guard for two seconds, had a meal with a Salvo, and look what had happened. She'd really lost it. She raised her head and everything spun round. She wasn't used to medication anymore. While she was on loads of antidepressants and Modecate she didn't get angry, and the voices went away, but who wanted to go through life doped up to the eyeballs? What the hell was wrong with her?

She wasn't schizo. Sir Harold, the old guy in the cream

suit, now that was schizo, slipping in and out of reality with delusions that he was the Son of God. That was really schizo. She was normal, except for the voices that came when she got scared or angry. Once she got rid of them, she'd be okay. No, not normal, she had a high IQ. Did people with high IQs hear voices in their heads? She'd never thought to ask the shrinks.

Carefully Larceny sat up, pushed back the covers, and swung her legs out of the bed onto the floor. She sat there for a moment till her head stopped spinning. She knew where her clothes would be, in the narrow cupboard beside the bed. She'd been in enough hospitals to know the routine. The cupboard squeaked as she opened it. In the darkness her searching fingers found her clothes, shoes, and the coat. Good. Even her tote bag was there. One of the cops must've picked it up, or maybe Kevin. No matter, it was here safe and sound.

Amazing. No guards, no nurse on duty. They were either very slack, thinking she was out for the count, or very busy. Cautiously she got dressed. She slipped on her sneakers, hoisted her bag over her arm, and crept out the door and along the passage. There were two nurses in the station, one writing something and one on the phone. Bending over double, Larceny slid along the wall, out of their sight. She got to the end of the passage. An elevator? Or the stairs. No choice, an elevator could attract attention. She sneaked down the stairs, holding on to the banister for support.

Reaching the next level, she paused for breath. Moans and sighs drifted through the hospital darkness as humans turned and tossed in their restless sleep. Down more stairs. Keeping to the wall, she moved like a shadow to the entrance. The magnetic doors slid silently back, and she slipped through like a haunted being, ghostly in her long coat, her feet making no sound on the steps.

Without looking back, she set off up Commercial Road. She'd tried the down-side of town before. Now she was heading uptown to whatever fate was going to dish out this time.

So much for God and the Salvos.

ten

LARCENY kept walking and walking. The rain had eased to a fine drizzle. She didn't know where she was going, and she didn't really care, for there was nowhere to go. Wherever she went she took herself, and there was no escape.

Her legs ached as she walked along roads, down streets and along more roads. She wasn't going back to Flinders Street Station: Every time she hit that place something bad happened. She just wanted to find a hole, crawl into it, and be left alone. She hated herself and, therefore, hated everyone else.

Eventually she just couldn't walk any farther and slumped down on a bench in a busy shopping center. People bustled past, intent on their business, oblivious to the girl in the Dri-as-a-Bone sitting in the drizzling rain. Or, if some of them did see her, they ignored her. They didn't want to get involved.

Head down, looking at the swirling water in the gutter,

Larceny was aware that the seat moved slightly. Someone had sat down next to her. She slid a glance from under her hood.

The person was wearing a hooded jacket, jeans, and Blundstones. It was hard to tell whether it was a male or female. The person was hunched over, staring at the space between the Blundstones. Suddenly, a quick look was directed at Larceny, catching her unaware. It was a woman.

"Shit of a day," she said.

"Yeah."

"A hot-soup sort of day."

"Yeah. Right."

Larceny was immediately aware that she hadn't had breakfast. She looked at her watch. It was past two. Her stomach growled with hunger. She had money, if the hospital crew hadn't nicked it. She felt in her pocket, and her groping fingers found the notes rolled tightly at the bottom of her pocket. Good. She'd get something to eat.

Abruptly she stood up. The woman stood up, too.

"There's a good place just down the street," she said, as if she could read Larceny's mind. "Come on, I'll show you."

"I don't need . . ."

But the woman was striding off without a backward glance. She seemed to be assuming that Larceny would follow her. Well, she could get stuffed, said Larceny's brain, but her feet unwillingly followed the woman down the street and into a café.

"Hang your coat up here," said the woman, shedding her jacket and hanging it up on a coat stand. Larceny did the same, and hung the tote bag over the top.

"Over here."

She sat down at a table near the window. Larceny followed and sat, too. Without the hood hiding her face Larceny could now see that she was younger than she'd first thought, maybe late twenties. She had straight black hair which was obviously dyed because the roots were a mousy brown. She had a nose ring and a series of rings along each earlobe. Her face, devoid of any cosmetics, was open and friendly. Gray eyes surveyed Larceny calmly.

"Like I said, a shit of a day. They make good pumpkin soup here."

The waitress came up to take the order.

"Pumpkin soup, and I'll have the vegetarian focaccia. Oh, and a mineral water. Thanks."

A health nut, thought Larceny, looking at the menu. The pumpkin soup sounded good, but she didn't want this woman to think she could be easily influenced. She'd make up her *own* mind, pay for her own food.

"I'll have the minestrone, um . . . and the Volcano pizza with double salami, please. And a coffee."

"Espresso, cappuccino?"

"Just flat white, thanks."

"And can we have some herb bread, too?" said the woman.

Larceny noted the "we" and was determined not to eat the herb bread. She looked defiantly at her and saw amusement lurking in the gray eyes.

"So. A bad day to be out in the rain," she said. "A bad day all round."

"Yeah?"

Larceny didn't want to hear about someone else's problems: She had enough of her own.

"I meant a bad day for you."

"Huh?"

Larceny looked wary. What did she mean? How did she know Larceny was having a bad day? Was she a cop? Cops didn't usually wear nose rings, but then if they were undercover . . . or was she from a hospital? Or a psych ward?

"You don't look happy," said the woman.

"So? Is that a crime?"

She shrugged as the waitress put a basket of hot herb bread on the table. The smell made Larceny's mouth water. The woman took a piece and bit into it, the herb butter dribbling onto her chin. She wiped it off with the back of her hand and nudged the basket toward Larceny.

"Have some. It's good."

She looked out the window and kept munching. Larceny fought a quick internal battle and lost. She grabbed a piece and took a huge bite. Often after medication she was ravenous. Most people lost their appetites, but she never did. The bread was delicious. She glanced at the woman, but she was still street-gazing, so she took another piece, and yet another. Then the woman looked back.

"I'm Kaz," she said.

Larceny kept quiet. She was sick and tired of telling strangers her name. Telling anyone anything. She stared resolutely at the bread basket.

"You have lovely hair," said Kaz. "Mine's always a mess. I've tried being blond, red, and now black. What do you think?"

"Why don't you leave it? Have your own color!"

"But it's so drab. Mousy brown. In my line of work I have to look dramatic."

Larceny was sucked in before she realized it.

"What work?"

"I'm an outreach worker."

Larceny tensed.

"Relax. I'm not a psychologist or a social worker, I just cruise round and talk to young people."

"Sounds a snap of a job," said Larceny sarcastically. She'd met youth workers who'd wanted her to join mental workshops, play netball, do outdoor adventures, which were pissy. Some were government ones, some were religious ones attached to churches, but they were all pains in the neck.

The soup arrived, steaming in thick brown bowls. The

pumpkin *did* look really good, better than the minestrone. Kaz noted her look but didn't say anything, just started calmly spooning up her soup. They ate in silence.

Larceny was puzzled. Usually youth workers sort of bubbled idiotically all over her, nervously eager to please, to get her sorted out, to get some gold stars on their Good Works charts. This one was different. This one was laid-back and cool. Kaz was getting to her. By not doing anything she was beginning to really confuse her! No bright, breezy approach. No psychobabble or social-work jargon. Nothing.

"Larceny," said Larceny suddenly.

"Excuse me?"

"My name."

"Oh. Right. Good, here's the focaccia and your pizza."

Kaz started in on the focaccia bread. Larceny kept staring at her.

"What? Have I got parsley in my teeth or something?"

"No. It's just that . . . when are you going to start in with the questions?"

"What questions?"

"Who are you? Where are you going? What do you want to do in five years' time? Why are you doing this? All that sort of shit."

"Do you want me to ask those questions?"

"No."

"Okay. I won't. Your pizza's getting cold."

The room hummed with noisy conversation, washing

over Larceny like a warm and soothing comforter. Normal people having normal conversations with each other as they ate normal food.

"What *is* normal?" she blurted out.

"I dunno. You tell me."

"Normal people don't hear voices in their heads," said Larceny, looking carefully at Kaz to see if she'd flinch, back away, or look scared. Kaz didn't move a muscle.

"Who says?"

"Everyone says."

"Who's everyone?"

"You know!" Larceny scrunched up her paper napkin as the waitress brought the coffee and mineral water. "Doctors. Psychs. Shrinks. Cops. Youth workers!"

She spat the last word defiantly. Kaz just gazed back at her, mild interest on her face.

"Maybe no one's normal," she said. "Maybe we're all abnormal except for people who hear voices, and maybe they're normal."

"You're nuts!" exclaimed Larceny.

"See? Now you think I'm nuts. It's all very subjective, isn't it?"

"I don't get you at all."

"That's okay, most people don't," said Kaz, dragging out a packet of cigarettes. She offered one to Larceny.

"Excuse me, no smoking," said the waitress.

"Whoops, sorry. I forgot." She looked at Larceny. "We'll have to smoke outside."

"I'm fifteen," said Larceny. "Don't you know it's illegal to give smokes to underage kids?"

"Whoops, sorry. I forgot," said Kaz, with a gleam in her eyes. "Let's pay the bill and go outside. Go you halves, Larceny."

"You can call me Larce. And what if I haven't got any money?"

"You have. But if you don't want to spend it, I can live with that."

Larceny dragged out a crumpled ten. The waitress gave her change from her share of the bill. A dollar.

"One thing about Burgermania, you get more for your money," she said under her breath, as she collected her coat and tote bag. Kaz frowned but said nothing.

They went outside. Kaz lit up a smoke without offering one, then dropped the packet on the ground. She started to walk away.

"Your cigarettes."

Larceny bent and retrieved them.

"Finders keepers," said Kaz, and kept walking. Larceny grinned. This Kaz was smart. Legally she couldn't offer cigarettes, so she'd found a way round it. But it was unnecessary: Larceny had her own supply.

"Here."

She shoved the packet into Kaz's hand and dragged out her own.

"Where are we going?" she asked.

"I dunno. Where do you want to go?"

Larceny shrugged. "I dunno. Take in a movie. Play some pool. Fill in time."

"Ah, yes. Filling in time. Not easy when there's days, weeks, years of it."

Kaz stopped at a newsstand. She bought a paper. Tucking it under her arm, she fell into step beside Larceny. "Game of pool, then?"

"Yeah. Why not?"

Kaz led the way down the street to a billiard parlor called The Pot Room, and they went in. As usual it was dimly lit, and as usual there were people hanging round playing pool, talking, playing the machines, and generally filling in time. She put her money on the corner of the table, and they sat down. Larceny had a quick glance round as Kaz flipped through the paper. She couldn't see anyone she knew. Good! Then several young people spotted Kaz and cruised over.

"Ty's gone. He found out his brother's in Perth."

"Thanks for letting me know, Elise."

"I need money, Kaz."

"Have you tried the court? You'll have to take this form down there."

She scribbled down some details. "There could be some money: It's after two, so they'll have heard some cases." She looked at Larceny. "The poor box. People have to pay into it," she explained.

"I know."

Not that Larceny had ever used it. It went against her

values, ripping off the poor to pay the poor. A lot of the contributors were losers: She didn't want money from losers. But the rich were fair game. The big stores, the homes of the rich and famous, though burgs weren't really her line. Shoplifting was fair: They had stacks of gear in those stores, plenty of money. She was entitled to nick the stuff. Wasn't she?

The problem with living in foster care and homes was that you got so many rules crammed into your head you couldn't possibly obey them all. Easy rules to obey, like, "Don't chew with your mouth open," and "Tidy your room." Hard ones, like, "The world doesn't owe you anything." As far as Larceny was concerned, the world owed her a lot!

"No," Kaz was saying to a young guy with dreadlocks and a checked shirt about three sizes too big. "You know I can't give out money. If you need food, I can give you a voucher. Have you seen Gina lately?"

"Nah."

"I thought you were going to join the peer Ed group?"

"Changed me mind, like."

"Okay. Oh, great, the pool table's free. Come on, Larce, let's see if you can wield a mean cue."

"Hey, Kaz, is it the peer Ed group today?" The guy with the checked shirt tugged at her arm.

"Yes. Three-thirty till five."

"Got nothin' else to do. Might as well go."

"Okay. Catch you later. Have a good one."

Kaz picked up her cue and chalked the end.

"You can break."

Larceny liked pool. She was good at it, having played it in countless rec rooms. Bang. The balls rolled across the green baize of the table. Beautifully set up for some good shots. Kaz potted one, then missed. Larceny grinned, and with ease potted ball after ball.

"Okay, okay. What about a game of tennis or golf?" said Kaz, shaking her head in despair.

"It's years since I played tennis," said Larceny, thinking of the Wilsons and how every person of any Wilson worth to the community had to be able to "play a good game of tennis." She'd never touched a racquet since!

"Kaz. I think I've got scabies," said a skinny kid who looked about nine. "I reckon I got them off Kylie and Kris. They told me you said they had scabies."

"Where, Joey? Show me."

"Here."

Kaz peered at his arm. "Looks more like flea bites to me. Are you still living in that place with all the cats?"

"Yeah."

"I'll see if I can get you some spray to kill fleas, and some lotion for your bites. Can you come to the office round, say, four?"

Kaz kept getting besieged by kids wanting this and that. How she kept her cool Larceny wasn't sure, but she treated each one with sincerity and respect, however dumb their requests sounded.

"You're too bloody good to be true, St. Kaz of Pool," she said, when one girl had been bitching for ten minutes about another girl and Kaz had patiently listened.

"Yeah? Were you in Burgermania last night?"

Wham, right between the eyes, catching Larceny off guard so that her mouth dropped open in shock.

"Who, me?"

"Yes, you."

"What if I was?"

She was very defensive, muscles tensed, ready to run, the haunted look back in her eyes.

"Just asking, that's all. It was on the radio this morning. And it's in the paper."

Kaz passed it over. Larceny swiftly scanned the page. The press had beefed it up, making her sound like a total maniac! There was a full description down to the coat and tote bag, and a photo of Kevin standing next to Katie, both looking concerned, anxious, and squeaky clean.

"Nah, not me. Another chick with a bad attitude, man."

Kaz glanced at her watch. "It's nearly four, and I have to get back to the office. Do you want to come with me?"

"Do I have a choice?"

Kaz looked puzzled. "Of course you have a choice. You can do what you like."

"I thought you might get me there, then call the cops."

Kaz smiled. "If I called the cops every time some young

person in trouble or with a warrant out on them cruised in, I'd have no young people, and I'd be out of a job."

Larceny sighed. She was so tired. Life seemed to consist of a few warm baths, some food, then rain, cold, and loneliness. She knew that she couldn't keep running forever. But when she did stop and try to get it together, something always stuffed it up. Other people, other kids, being in the wrong place at the wrong time. And the voices. She wondered in a moment of mad panic if she shot herself in the head, shot them, would they still keep taunting her even after she was dead?

"Coming?" Kaz was putting on her coat.

"Yeah. Right. Why not?"

Kaz shared an office across from The Pot Room with several other youth workers. It was a typical youth-worker office, old furniture and desks, a couple of sagging sofas, a café bar on one wall with a sign SORRY. OUT OF HOT CHOC., scraggy carpeting that had seen better days, and posters all over the walls saying "If it's not on, it's not on," "Kid's Assist," "Magical Medicos—a free clinic for young people," "Eat Healthy, Live to be Wealthy," and "Quit! While You're Ahead!" There were the usual pamphlets about youth services—accommodation, jobs, health clinics, legal services, studying out of school, adventure camps, hobbies . . .

"Have you ever wondered why kids are on the street when there's all this lovely stuff to do?" said Larceny with mock innocence.

One of the youth workers, an earnest-looking young guy who looked like he'd be more at home driving the community bus or shooting at hoops, pressed his lips together. Kaz just laughed.

"You know as well as I do, Larce, that we keep getting it wrong. But what else are we s'posed to do with not enough money, not enough time, and not enough cooperation from parents, teachers, traders, and the law?"

There was a babble of voices from an adjoining room.

"Peer Ed," said Kaz, raising her eyes to the roof. "You want to sit in for a while? I've got some serious paperwork to do and phone calls to make."

Larceny sighed. Peer Ed sounded boringly educational. She hovered uncertainly near the doorway, unsure of whether to join the group or split. Five guys, including Joey, the skinny kid in the too-big checked shirt, and three girls were arguing the point with each other and one of the leaders.

"We wanna do the horse riding, Lisa," yelled Joey.

"If you choose horse riding and dolphin watching I should be able to organize it fairly quickly," the leader said, raising her voice above the racket. She was a large girl with short dark hair, wearing what looked like a gray blanket tied with a piece of woven leather round her middle. "If you want to run a dance party, someone has to organize the venue, the band, the caterer, and the tickets."

Larceny had heard it all before. The leaders would let

the kids think that they were running the thing, but would have their own adult agendas. The kids would be made to do the organizing, supposedly to teach them responsibility and decision-making. It was crap. This leader wanted horses and dolphins: She was going to lay the call and make it too hard for them to do a dance party.

"Go for the dance party," Larceny said loudly from the doorway.

"Who are you?" The woman glared.

"Who cares? I'm saying the dance party." She pointed at the youth worker. "Make her work for her money!"

She decided to bail out. This wasn't her scene at all. She sauntered through the office toward the door. Kaz saw her, put down the phone, and grabbed her coat from the back of her chair.

"Let's go."

"I thought you had to make phone calls and do paperwork."

"I can do the calls later on the mobile and the paperwork can wait. Time to go home."

"But . . ."

"You do want to go home, don't you?"

Home. It was so long ago that Larceny had a real home that for a moment she panicked. Home. Four walls that were not barred or guarded. Shit. Could she cope?

eleven

KAZ lived in a tiny house in a side lane. It was old and preloved, with a tangle of rosebushes crowding for space along the front fence and a sagging front verandah that needed some serious repair work. Kaz unlocked the door, and they went in. It was like a little granny cottage with a passage straight down the middle and rooms to either side.

"I hope you like cats," she said, as a gray Persian-cross stalked majestically up to Larceny and started winding himself round her legs.

"I love cats. And dogs."

"Good. This is Sir Tom. And you have to meet Reuben the Rotty," Kaz said, leading the way down a short passage to the back door, opening it, and letting in this huge slobbering rottweiler.

"Won't he eat the cat?"

"No. They were brought up together. Fur brothers. Now, I'll show you your bedroom."

It was a tiny room at the back of the house with a single bed, wardrobe, chest of drawers, and a wooden chair with spindly legs. The bed was covered with a bright blue comforter, with pink-and-green scatter cushions thrown haphazardly on it. There were posters of Silverchair on the wall. A bunch of roses in a chipped blue jar sat on the chest of drawers, sweetening the air with their strong perfume. On a wooden chair was a pile of clothing, and shoes, socks, and panty hose littered the floor. It looked and smelled like a happy, lived-in, and loved room.

"Diana's usually in here, but she's away at a conference," said Kaz, kicking the assortment of footwear and hose under the bed and tossing the clothes in a jumbled heap in a drawer.

"I thought youth workers weren't allowed to take in kids," said Larceny.

"It's not policy, but it's not encouraged either. Anyway, I do as I like. Sometimes I take in young people when they need a place for a night or two. Do you want to do some washing?"

Larceny frowned. She had a plastic bag. Now where . . . ? Lynx's place. It seemed like years ago.

"No."

"Okay. Come in the kitchen and I'll cook up something. I don't suppose you are a Cordon Bleu chef in disguise by any chance? I hate cooking."

"I'm okay at pasta."

"Great. Do what you will with pasta, and I'll do a salad."

Larceny felt peaceful for the first time in ages as she boiled the pasta, fried bacon pieces, diced onions, and grated some cheese for her masterpiece. There was something soothing about cooking. Kaz didn't chatter; she silently went about washing lettuce leaves and slicing up tomato, cucumber, and green pepper. It was a companionable silence, not an awkward, uneasy one. The kitchen was small but had a cheerful air about it. Some copper pans hung above the stove, and there were some big pottery jars on a shelf. Other glass jars held various herbs and spices. Red tea towels hung on a railing, and two brightly patterned aprons hung on a hook. It was a comfortably cluttered mixture of old and new.

"It's ready," said Larceny, pouring the cheese sauce over the steaming fettucine she'd drained in a colander and put onto two warmed china plates.

"Want to eat by the TV? Hang on, I'll have to put Sir Tom and Reuben out or they'll practically climb down your throat for the food."

The animals were put outside, and they carried their plates of fettucine, cutlery, and the bowl of salad into the family room.

"Oh! Cooool!" said Larceny.

A whole sideboard was devoted to crystals and rocks of all shapes and sizes. There were jars of feathers everywhere, dream catchers hanging from the ceiling and posters of wolves on the walls.

"What's with the wolves?"

"They're my guardians," said Kaz.

Larceny wasn't sure whether she was joking or not.

"I'm sort of into oneness," explained Kaz, dumping the bowl of salad on the coffee table, sinking into a fat leather armchair, and indicating that Larceny should sit in the other armchair.

"Huh?"

"We're all one and the same."

"Yeah, right. I really feel like I'm a lump of pink crystal or a feather or a wolf!"

"Maybe one day you will if you're lucky."

Was Kaz joking or not? It was hard to tell. Maybe she was nuts. Nah, youth workers weren't nuts, they were screened before they were trained and let loose on the general public. Balancing her plate on her knees, Larceny twirled some fettucine on her fork.

"You wouldn't want to be in oneness with me," she said. "I'm bad. And most people think I'm mad!"

"Yeah? Who says?"

"A million social workers, shrinks, doctors, teachers, and cops, that's who."

"Why should they think you're mad?"

"I hear voices. I want to hurt people, sometimes even kill them," said Larceny, keeping her eyes on her plate. She was too scared to see Kaz's reaction, too scared to be rejected, ejected out of this nice warm house with the friendly vibes.

"Is that what happened in Burgermania?"

"It was this bloody Salvo," said Larceny, feeling her anger begin to rise at the thought of Kevin telling her she should give God a chance. "He said I was one of God's children. What's God ever done for me?"

"How are you feeling right now?"

"Angry!"

Larceny put down her plate. She waited for the gray mists to come swirling, cowering back against the dark forces that took over her mind, the voices that took over her will. Nothing happened. She blinked.

"No voices!" she said in awe. "It must be this room."

"Or maybe the sedatives they gave you last night have calmed you down," said Kaz. "Maybe it'd be a good idea to stay on them until you work through your anger and learn to manage negative feelings in a better way."

"And maybe you should shut up with the psych shit!"

"You're right. Sorry." Kaz helped herself to the salad. "Want some?"

"In a minute. How did you know I was given sedatives last night?"

"I do have certain responsibilities in my job, Larce. The cops were searching for you all over the city."

"There's a warrant out?" Larceny tensed.

"No. They were worried about your safety. So were the hospital staff."

"Oh, sure. There's all these loonies out of their heads wandering round the streets because the government's shut down a heap of mental homes and psych wards, and they're worrying about me? Forget it. They only want to lock me up before I kill someone. They couldn't give a shit about my safety. Anyway, you can tell them all from me that they don't have to worry. I can look after myself. I don't need their help, and I don't need your help!"

She jumped up, flinging her arms about in her agitation. One hand caught on a dream catcher and the feathers went whirling round and round like a spinning top.

"It's okay," said Kaz. "I'm not going to help you. I'm eating your fettucine and letting you sleep in Diana's bed, that's all."

Larceny sat back on the sofa, looking suspicious.

"Who's this Diana?"

"My friend."

"Are you a lezzo?"

"No. I don't give myself a brand name like a box of soap powder."

"But do you sleep with her?"

"No. I live with her."

"Do you sleep with anyone, then?"

"Yes, myself and about half a million stuffed teddies and gorillas."

"You don't sleep with guys?"

"I'm not in any sort of sexual relationship at the moment," said Kaz. "I'm too bloody tired from sorting out the sexual confusions of the rest of the population to be even vaguely interested."

"Well, say you had really bad sex with a guy—no a couple of guys, and then, say, you had good sex with a girl, does that mean you're gay? A lezzo?"

"No, it just means you had bad sex with two guys and good sex with a girl."

"You need to speak to Comma," said Larceny with satisfaction. "The stupid slut's being taken for a ride in more ways than one."

"But on the other hand, she could be gay," said Kaz.

"How's she s'posed to know, then?"

"It'll feel right."

"That's crazy. How can you know what's right unless you do it, and then if it's wrong, you'll feel lousy for the rest of your life?" yelled Larceny.

"If you make a mistake, it doesn't mean you have to feel guilty for the rest of your life. Mistakes are part of learning about life, and different people learn different things in different ways. But guilt and shame are such negative emotions. Do you know that there are two kinds of shame, Larceny? There's healthy shame—like your conscience that tells you you've done something wrong, something unlawful. And then there's toxic shame. That's all your childhood crap you've had dumped on you by your parents or stepparents or foster parents or teachers or whoever. But you can't blame them because they had stuff dumped on them by their parents, and their parents, and so on down the line back to Adam and Eve."

"Not that religious Adam and Eve thing again," snorted Larceny. "I've sat through a million sermons on the Garden of Eden and the Tree of Life. It was a real stupid setup. If it hadn't been Eve who ate the apple, it would've been someone else. Some dumb chick would'vc had a bite of that apple eventually, or some even dumber guy. The sins of the fathers and all that—"

"The point is that this toxic shame is poisonous stuff. It eats into you and destroys you so much that you begin to believe you're a worthless mistake. And it destroys any chance of having a decent, honest relationship with another person. We've all got some toxic shame, but some people have got more than others. We all have to learn to deal with it in order to feel happy."

"Yeah? This is just religious crap!"

"No, Larce, it's life!"

Larceny screwed up her face in concentration. This toxic-shame idea. It made sense. She'd felt worthless as long as she could remember.

"I've got a high IQ," she blurted out.

"Are you pleased about that?"

Kaz was clever. She hadn't asked who said it, why Larce had been tested, how the tests were done, where, when, and what for. She'd sort of turned it round.

"I dunno. Hasn't done me much good except get me into trouble."

"But you seem pleased to tell me that you've got a high IQ."

"It's the only thing I've got," said Larceny simply.

Then to her astonishment she found herself pouring out her life story: It usually had to be pried out of her, and then she only ever revealed the bits she wanted to share. Kaz sat and listened. She was a very unusual person. Most adults immediately tried to tell you what to do, when to do, and how to do it. Kaz didn't interrupt at all: She just listened. Eventually Larceny ran out of words. She felt drained, like someone had pulled the plug and let her life go seeping through the carpet.

"Want some coffee?"

Larceny nodded, too worn-out to speak. Kaz went into the kitchen. While she was rattling cups, Larceny could hear her talking to her animals as she fed them. Then Reuben and Sir Tom came marching in with Kaz, both looking indignant. They'd been out in the cold for hours. They stretched side by side near the fire and fell asleep as Kaz put down two mugs.

"Milk, no sugar."

"How did you remember?"

"I always remember the important things in life, and milk, no sugar equals Larceny!"

"Yeah. This toxic-waste stuff . . ."

"Toxic shame."

"If you think you've got it, how do you get rid of it?"

"Well, the most important thing is to realize you've

got it, and it's not your fault. Then you probably need some sort of counseling to help you deal with it."

"No way. No counseling! All that's ever done is stuff me up completely, made me feel worse."

"The techniques are improving all the time. It depends who's doing the counseling, of course."

"No!"

"There's some books and videotapes by an American guy called John Bradshaw. If you read the books, they'll help you understand yourself and help you get rid of toxic shame."

"Have you got rid of yours?"

"I'm working on it, Larce, I'm working on it." Kaz yawned. "I'm afraid I'm going to have to call it a night, Larce. It's nearly twelve, and I have to be up by seven. I've put on your electric blanket, and the bathroom's just across from your room if you want a shower. Sleep tight."

It was years since anyone had said, "Sleep tight." One of the foster mums; she couldn't remember which one. Her life was a mish-mash of different family values, sayings, customs, and habits.

"Yeah. 'Night."

Larceny went into the bathroom and washed her face and hands. She stripped off her clothes and rinsed out her underwear so it'd be dry in the morning. If it wasn't, she could run the hair dryer over it, an old trick she'd learned on the streets when she'd dried her undies under the hand dryers in public toilets.

Looking round, Larceny decided it was the most unusual bathroom she'd ever seen. Someone (probably Kaz) had stuck up all these postcards, stickers, articles torn from magazines, and photocopied poems and sayings. All were positive. "Trust in yourself." "Today is the first day of the rest of your life." "Today is the day you were worrying about yesterday." "Smile and be happy." None of them seemed religious: no mention of God. Larceny came to the conclusion that Kaz was running her own breed of religion with her crystal collection and her visually positive bathroom.

Her bed was lovely, warm and cozy, the mattress slightly saggy so that it folded round her like a cocoon. She should've been dog-tired but amazingly was wide-awake. She went over in her mind about what Kaz had said. Toxic shame? She could invent a whole list of toxics. Toxic love. Toxic hate. Toxic greed. Toxic envy. Toxic lust. Toxic power. Could you have toxic guilt and anger?

Kaz didn't seem like a religious nut. Apart from crystals, feathers, and wolves she seemed cool. Maybe she'd let her stay for a while. It would be nice to have a safe place without someone trying to unscramble her head. Maybe Kaz had been trying to unscramble her head, but at least it wasn't intrusive. Or uncomfortable. Or threatening. She fell asleep to the comfortable tick-tock of Diana's alarm clock near the bed, her first naturally deep and peaceful sleep for a long time.

"Wake up. Breakfast's ready."

Kaz stood in the doorway with a towel wrapped round her head. Larceny blinked. Where was she? Who was this weirdo wearing a pink turban?

Then she remembered where she was and sat bolt upright.

"I meant to get up early."

"What for?"

"I dunno. I thought I could make you some toast or something."

Larceny felt confused. She seldom ever offered to do anything for anyone. Even making the fettucine the night before had been a rare occurrence. Maybe Kaz had sprayed the walls with weird drugs that made a person feel comfy and eager to please. Or maybe it was just Kaz.

She swung her legs out of bed.

"Oh, hell," said Kaz. "You're wearing your T-shirt. I never thought to get you a nighty or PJs. Hang on, I'll get you a dressing gown. You can try wearing Diana's slippers, but she's got feet like kayaks. They'll probably fall off your feet."

Kaz disappeared and came back with an old faded blue chenille robe that had seen better days.

"Here you go. It's practically an antique, but it's clean."

Breakfast was stewed apples, toast with honey, and coffee.

"I'd like you to come with me, Larce. I've got a couple of kids who are in deep shit, and I think you could help them," Kaz said as she drained the last of her coffee.

"Me? Help someone? Get real, Kaz, I can't even get my own shit together."

"You'll be surprised how useful you'll be. Trust me!"

twelve

LARCENY ran down the road, her tote bag banging wildly against her hip. Ducking down an alley, she weaved along the narrow one-way thoroughfare before bursting onto another main road. Cars zoomed past, their drivers in a hurry to get to work before the peak hour slowed them to a snail's-pace crawl. Her lungs bursting, screaming for air, she panted to a stop, heaving in great gulps of misty morning smog.

"Trust me," Kaz had said.

They'd got to the office, only been there minutes, when two cops had arrived, a male and a female. Kaz had done a great acting job feigning surprise: She could've won an Oscar, she was so convincing. The babe from peer Ed in the gray blanket thing had stood there smirking like a fat slimy slug.

"Are you Larceny Leyton?" the female cop had asked.

Larceny had been too choked up with shock, betrayal, and anguish to answer. She'd just stared at Kaz with bleak hatred.

"I didn't have anything to do with this," Kaz had argued, as the other cop took out his notebook. "You only have to give them your name and address. You have rights, Larce."

"Address? Should I give them yours?" Larceny had spat, her eyes flashing with rage. She'd begun to tremble, she was so angry at herself for getting conned. To trust Kaz and get kicked in the teeth yet again. It was too much. With a savage cry she'd swept her arm across Kaz's desk, knocking the phone and papers flying before whirling for the door.

"Get her," yelled the cop with the notebook.

The female cop had lunged after her, but when Larceny was in flight mode she was as slippery as an eel. She twisted out of reach and pounded out the door, her long legs carrying her rapidly down the street. She could hear Kaz shouting at the cops and shouting for her to come back, but it was all mixed up. She'd done what she always did when there was trouble with the law—run like hell. Kaz's voice still echoed in her head. "I didn't turn you in. It was Lisa. I didn't. I wouldn't. Trust me, Larceny. Please!"

Larceny sighed. She'd really panicked at the refuge. Kaz had said she hadn't turned her in, it was that other bitch. Maybe she should go back. Yes. She would. Right now!

A black shiny car pulled alongside.

"Are you all right?" asked this middle-aged guy in a business suit, winding down his window.

No. It was too scary to go back. What if Kaz was angry with her for running off? What if she rejected her? She couldn't take the chance. Larceny looked at the driver.

"Something bad's happened. I have to get to my mum," she lied.

"Should I call the police? I've got my mobile."

"No. If I could just get a ride to the city . . ."

She climbed into the front seat and he smoothly pulled back into the traffic. He had his radio tuned in to some classical-music station. She hoped the cops didn't broadcast an APB.

"What happened? Did someone hurt you?" asked the man, driving fast toward the city. Larceny wished he'd slow down. It'd be just her lousy luck for him to get pulled over for speeding.

"My stepdad. He . . . well . . . you know . . . he . . ."

Larceny pretended to burst into tears. She was brilliant at spinning shit. She'd been doing it for years.

"Are you sure you don't want the police?"

"No. I want my mum."

"Where's her office, dear?"

"In Flinders Street, near the station."

"All right, we'll be there soon."

His idea of soon and Larceny's idea of soon were light-years apart. All she wanted to do was jump on the first train to some remote country town. No, wait. She'd be better back in the city: She'd be harder to find, then. Get some black hair dye, visit the Ladies'—no one would be looking for a girl with short black hair, 'cause she'd buy some scissors and hack it off. Get rid of the jacket, nick something less obvious. Junk the tote bag. Pity, it was her lucky bag. But then maybe it was unlucky. It'd never brought her good fortune, had it? There were real advantages in having a high IQ. Real advantages.

He turned into St. Kilda Road: The traffic was creeping along like a giant slug. The man was talking to her, and she hadn't been listening.

"Sorry. What did you say?"

"I'll park the car and come with you," he was saying.

That's what you think, she thought. The traffic moved then stopped again.

"Thanks for the ride, mister."

She wrenched open the car door and was out onto the road, running down the sidewalk and round a corner. She'd double back when she thought it was safe. He'd be stuck in the traffic, could only turn left. She'd be back onto St. Kilda Road before he had time to go round the block. She'd cross over the road. He had no hope of seeing her with four lanes of traffic as a shield.

Fear and anger always gave her extra energy. She felt as if she was invincible. She was Larceny Leyton. She could conquer the world. She sped back out onto St. Kilda Road, catching the lights near the Shrine. Maybe she could hide in there? No, best back at the station, get a train to the suburbs, disappear for a while. The crafty feral was taking over, planning, plotting with a raw native cunning. A high IQ and native cunning: She'd beat them all yet.

She slowed to a walk. Running attracted too much attention unless you were dressed for it, and she wasn't. She reached the bridge and crossed back over with the lights.

Flinders Street Station was home. It smelled safe and secure, the smell of sweat, grease, and grime of human bodies, engines, food, and machines far sweeter to her nostrils than the traitorous scent of roses.

She found her familiar spot against the wall and paused to get her breath. Looking at her watch, she saw that it was ten to nine. Good. The shops would be open then, and she could nick the scissors and the hair dye, and . . .

"Well, well, well. We meet again!"

Her blood froze. She knew that voice. Nick Farino.

She looked up defiantly. His shrewd eyes took in her blotchy, tear-stained face and drawn, haunted expression. He smiled to himself. He had her where he wanted her, vulnerable and helpless. She was a wild one all right. She had half the cops in the city chasing their tails. But he knew she'd come back here. She had nowhere else to go. He had unfinished business with her. And future plans.

"Let's go."

"I'm not going anywhere with you."

"Oh yes you are, or I'll turn you over to the cops and they'll lock you up."

"You're bluffing."

"Who's going to defend you? They can do what they like. Who'd miss you? They could stamp DEAD on your records and how would anyone ever find out that you're still alive? Who would want to? You're bad news."

Larceny sagged against him as he propelled her through the exit and down the steps. As before his car was round the corner. How had he known she'd show up? He bundled her unresisting body in and shut the door.

"My bag!"

She'd left it back in the station.

"You won't need it."

He shot away from the curb down Flinders Street, turning left into Kings Way and round the block, getting straight into St. Kilda Road on the green light. Smoothly he drove up Domain Road and into Park Street. It was no use attempting to try and jump out: He had his hand on the power switch for the door locks. And if she did, where would she go? There was no place to run anymore.

They reached his apartment building, and he slid the car into his space.

"Pity the cops didn't get you at that youth workplace as instructed and bring you straight here," he said, as they went up to the third floor. "I guessed you'd head for the station. You're a nuisance: I had to leave my breakfast."

"You—the cops—"

"Money can buy all sorts of things."

"Kaz?"

"Who the hell's Kaz? Oh, you mean that dumpy little youth worker who looks like an Indian squaw? She knew nothing. The other one, what was her name, Lisa or Eliza or something, she turned you in. If you didn't go round upsetting people so much, you wouldn't get into trouble, would you?"

So Kaz had been telling the truth! Larceny felt a glow of happiness. She faced Nick confidently.

"What the hell do you want with me?"

He grabbed at her arm.

"Don't touch me," she protested, but the gray mists didn't come, and neither did the voices. Neither did the anger.

He dragged her through his door, limp like a rag doll, and along the hallway into the kitchen.

"You've interrupted my breakfast, so you may as well wait till I've finished."

He pushed her down onto one of the chairs.

"Don't move, or I'll tie you up."

Larceny blanched. She hated to be touched, but even more she hated to be tied up. Once one of her foster fathers had tied her to a chair and made her sit for hours till her arms cramped and she'd peed her pants. She couldn't remember which one. But how did Nick Farino know she was petrified to be tied up? Or was it a lucky guess?

He'd reheated his coffee in the microwave. He came

back and sat opposite her, gazing at her with a curious expression.

"Yes. You'll make a good model. Young, fresh, virginal, yet wild as a tiger."

"Model?"

"For my girlie mag. Tasteful nude shots."

"You can jump off a rock," yelled Larceny. "I'd rather be dead and buried than pose nude for you."

He smiled in approval.

"I do like your spirit," he said. "Pity you're so aggro."

He was taunting her. Teasing her. With cold certainty Larceny realized that he knew something about her . . .

"It must've come from your mother's side," he said. "She was always too fond of dope and LSD. Maybe you were affected in the womb?"

"What?"

"Your mother. I knew her. Very well."

"You knew my mother?"

Larceny's eyes were round in her face as she stared at the man across the table.

"Tess De Laville."

"That wasn't my mother. She was Tess Leyton."

But that was her father's name. Maybe that schizo Sir Harold had been right after all? Maybe she, Larceny Leyton of the red hair and green eyes so like Isadora Somebody was really related to a count and a countess? Maybe she was really a fabulously wealthy heiress? Maybe . . .

"As I said, I knew her very well!"

"Oh, yeah? Prove it."

"And I knew your father, Danny Leyton. He was a mate of mine."

He rubbed his hands together and beamed, but his eyes were mean. "He'd like to know that we've caught up, and that I'm going to take care of you. Because I will, Larceny. I will. I always take care of my girls. I've got three brothels, you know, all legal, and very lovely girls who know how to please my clients. And of course there's my photographic business, porn videos. They're a nice little earner. You'll have fun!"

"This has got to be some sick kind of joke. All this stuff about girlie mags, posing nude, and being a prostitute. We're on *Candid Camera,* right?"

She jumped to her feet, whirling round the room, her red hair flying out round her white face like a living flame, pulling faces, poking her tongue out, and rolling her eyes up into her head.

"Stop it!"

His voice was cutting, cold. His pupils were pinpricks, black and coldly violent.

"You reckon I'm wild," she panted as she backed against the sliding glass door. "Compared to you I'm tame. You're evil!"

He gave a low chuckle, and it wasn't mirthful, either. It was demonic. Larceny felt her skin crawl. He was evil. She felt for the handle of the door. She had to get out. Scream for help.

She flung back the sliding glass door with a crash. He stood there chuckling softly as she backed up against the balcony railing.

"Come near me and I'll jump," she shrieked.

"I don't think so. You won't jump. You haven't got the guts!"

She stared at him in terror. His eyes were so cold. Flecks of spittle were on his lips as he smiled. He was enjoying every moment.

She heaved herself up onto the railing.

"Stay away from me. I'll jump!"

"I hear that every day," he smirked. "People owing me rent. Girls wanting to get out of the game. My game. I take care of them, don't I?" He leered at her. "Come here, Larceny. I'm going to take care of you. You won't jump like your mother did, will you? But then you are your mother's daughter, my dear, and she was insane."

He smiled, taunting her. She looked at him, and her head swam. Her mother wasn't insane, just confused and desperate. Just as she was now.

Suddenly her thoughts were chillingly clear. And sane. No, she wasn't going to jump. Then he'd win. She was her mother's daughter, but history wasn't going to repeat itself. And she wasn't going to work for him, either. But he didn't know that. Yet.

She shrugged and stepped away from the balcony.

"Okay. You win!"

But he hadn't. She'd escape when his back was turned.

Or when he had her in the car. She'd run. But she wouldn't keep running like before. This time she had somewhere to go. Someone she could trust to help her get her life on track. Someone she should have trusted in the first place.

Kaz.

A fantasy, a love story, a summer of change...

The China Garden

By LIZ BERRY

AVON tempest

"Like a jewel box with hidden drawers and compartments, this finely crafted, multilayered novel holds many secrets...richly laden with mystery and suspense, in which the ordinary often masks unexpected interconnections and the extraordinary is natural to the story's wildly imagined terrain."
—PUBLISHERS WEEKLY ☆

CHN 0300